What others have said about
A Withered Nosegay:

NOEL COWARD

A WITHERED NOSEGAY
Three Cod Pieces

Carroll & Graf Publishers, Inc.
New York

Published by arrangement with Methuen London Ltd

First Carroll & Graf edition 1987

Carroll & Graf Publishers, Inc.
260 Fifth Avenue
New York, NY 10001

Library of Congress Cataloging-in-Publication Data

Coward, Noel, 1899–1973.
  A withered nosegay.

  1. Parodies.   I. Title.
PR6005.085W58   1987   823′.912   87-723
ISBN 0-88184-316-4 (pbk.)

Manufactured in the United States of America

Contents

Introduction

The three early works by Noël Coward included in this volume were originally published between 1922 and 1932. *A Withered Nosegay* was the first: *Spangled Unicorn*, last, with *Chelsea Buns* in between in 1925. All – with the exception of a recent American reprint of *Spangled Unicorn* – have been unavailable since their original publication. They are reproduced here in facsimile of the original editions.

A Withered Nosegay was written in 1921 and by the time of publication the following year, Noël was still only twenty-two and known solely through various stage appearances (since the age of eleven) and one produced play – *I'll Leave It To You*. The illustrations were undertaken by Lorn Macnaughtan, whom he met in 1919 and who was – as Lorn Loraine – to be Noël's friend and adviser until her death in 1967.

Around the period of writing *A Withered Nosegay* Noël decided the time had come to pay his first visit to New York. The trip meant that Noël made many new friends and acquaintances including Laurette Taylor (whose somewhat bizarre gatherings were later to inspire *Hay Fever*) and two people who were to become

his life-long friends – Alfred Lunt and Lynn Fontanne
He also succeeded in selling parts of *A Withered Nose-gay* to *Vanity Fair* magazine.

In 1922, *A Withered Nosegay* was also published in
America but in a slightly different form and under the
title *Terribly Intimate Portraits*. One reviewer remarked
that the book contained 'keen satire, kindly wit and
trenchant insight into the failings and foibles of people'
while another stated that 'the volume has a blithesome
spirit' (Noël might just possibly have read that one).

In London the following year (1923) Noël contri-
buted a sketch entitled *The Swiss Family Whittlebot* to
the revue *London Calling!* This caused one newspaper
to write, 'I hear that Edith Sitwell was very annoyed
at the Noël Coward burlesque of her and her brothers
in *London Calling!* and wrote a letter of protest after
reading the papers, winding up very cuttingly: "As I
shall be out of town for the next few days, I fear I shall
not have an opportunity of seeing the show." But
Miss Sitwell's estimate of the length of run has been
falsified, for *London Calling!* has already exceeded the
few days she gave it, and looks like being one of the
hits of the season.'

Noël, however, thoroughly enjoyed the Sitwell an-
noyance and took to devising paragraphs to get into
newspaper columns – for instance: 'Hernia Whittlebot, whose poems I quoted a short time ago, has now
turned her attention to Christmas card greetings. I

went to see her at the Duke of York's Theatre yesterday, where Mr Noël Coward explained that the poetess was resting after a heavy lunch which she had taken in order to attune her mind to the correct spirit of Christmas. One little thing which she dashed off after two helpings of pudding is called "Christmas Cheer." It runs:

> Snow and Pudding,
> Life and Death,
> Nothing,
> And yet Everything.
> For shame, Good
>   King Wenceslas!

Yet another which she evolved after coffee is prettily called "Caprice de Noël," and has all the elusive "something" of a genuine Whittlebot. Listen:

> Holly berries twinkle red;
> Oh! how red they are!
> Parlourmaids with cheeks aglow
> Scream beneath the mistletoe.
> Footmen, footmen, stuff your calves
> Wrapt in patriotic scarves;
> Portsmouth harbour, Portsmouth harbour,
> Dreams of Francis Drake.

Miss Whittlebot is busy preparing for publication her new books, *Gilded Sluts* and *Garbage*. She breakfasts on onions and Vichy water.'

Of course, Miss Whittlebot was not preparing either slim volume but Noël was busily preparing *Chelsea Buns*. Its 1925 publication prompted one critic to say, 'One almost feels sorry for Miss Sitwell, even though she has been, in the vernacular, "asking for it" for years.'

By the time *Spangled Unicorn* appeared in 1932, Noël was a world-famous figure. The years since *London Calling!* had seen a string of well-known and success-ful productions including: *The Vortex* (1924), *Fallen Angels, Hay Fever* and *On With the Dance* (1925), *The Marquise* and *Home Chat* (1927), *This Year of Grace!* (1928), *Bitter-Sweet* (1929), *Private Lives* (1930) and *Cavalcade* (1931).

Spangled Unicorn was for the most part well-received, with reviewers making such remarks as 'a wonderful piece of satire, a gorgeous display of literary fooling whose very subtlety increases our enjoyment.' How-ever, there was one area where the book was not well-regarded. As Sheridan Morley relates in his biography of Coward, *A Talent to Amuse:* 'To go with the cod biographies of his "poets", Noël used an unbeliev-able batch of old photographs which he had bought some years earlier in a London junkshop. But he had failed to realise that though the people involved would obviously now be dead, their families were still very much alive and not best pleased to find photographs of their dear departed adorning a mocking parody of this nature. It was with some difficulty and a certain amount of payment that he avoided actual lawsuits.'

MARTIN TICKNER

A
WITHERED NOSEGAY

COMPILED BY
NOEL COWARD

WITH
REPRODUCTIONS FROM OLD MASTERS BY
LORN MACNAUGHTAN

TO

ESME WYNNE-TYSON

THIS BOOK IS AFFECTIONATELY DEDICATED

AUTHOR'S NOTE

IN view of the fact that I have received many tiresome and even carping letters from the more captious critics of this child of my brain, I feel in justice to myself and Miss Macnaughtan that it is incumbent upon me to protest, in no measured terms, against what is not only an organised opposition and a pusillanimous display of superficial egotism, but a dirty trick.

I have been taunted with my inaccuracies : I have been called a fool ; an idiot ; an uneducated dolt ; and an illiterate cow ! This is far from kind, and I resent it.

My concentrated researches prove these memoirs to be absolutely accurate in every historical detail.

I refute utterly these criticisms, fostered by naught but the basest jealousy.

AUTHOR'S NOTE

My parents and other relatives consider the book excellent ; and anyhow, the published price is *not* high.

NOEL COWARD.

"THE HOLLIES,"
    MARINE CRESCENT,
        ROME.

CONTENTS

FOREWORD

THESE tender, intimate memoirs of the flower-like women who blossomed and bloomed when the world was young are the result of years of research in the National Archives, the Catacombs, and the Clapham Common Public Library.

No one can realise the work, the tireless energy, and concentration which are necessary in order to reconstruct—for a brief spell a moment here, five minutes there, in the multi-coloured lives of those glorious, flamboyant figures who flaunted and hurtled their way across the pages of History, leaving behind them an indescribable aroma of romance. Who are we to criticise these frail, lovely, yet withal earthly creatures—who are we to condemn their occasionally slightly irritating behaviour—who are we, anyhow ?

Ring up the curtain, and bring to life the dusty, jaded tapestries of yesterday—let us live once more

FOREWORD

the joys and sorrows, the laughter and tears, the
tragedy and comedy, the blood and thunder, that so
enlivened the lurid existences of long-dead ancestors. Let us dip our pen deep into the well of
truth, and endeavour to recapture for a fleeting
space the wistful echoes of past songs, the frou-frou
of brocaded skirts adown bygone corridors, and
withal the ineffable call of Romance and Daring
do—which, though dead to the world, may yet find
a faint response in the individual heart.

NOEL COWARD.

JULIE DE POOPINAC

From a Mezzotint by Mme. Tossele

A WITHERED NOSEGAY

JULIE DE POOPINAC

FOR several years all France rang with the name of Julie de Poopinac—or to give her her full title, Angelique Yvonne Mathilde Clementine Virginie Celeste Julie, Vicomtesse de Poopinac. As the most peerless of all the beauties at Court during the last years of a desperately tottering throne, she has been hailed and heralded (and is still in some outlying villages in Old Provence and Old Normandy) as almost an enchantress, so great was her beauty and her wit. Born in a stately chateau in Old Picardy, she was brought up in comparative seclusion ; her father, the Duc de Potache,[1] spent his time at Court, so that her radiant loveliness was left to mature and develop unnoticed. Her childhood

---

[1] Famous for being the means of introducing hornless cattle into the Gironde.

was uneventful, but at the age of seventeen this ravishing creature was wedded by proxy to Gustave de Poopinac, a dashing young officer in the Garde du Corps,[1] and at twenty-five she came to Court in order to see her husband ; but alas ! Fate, seated securely in Destiny's irreproachable turret, willed it that her journey should be in vain. She left Old Picardy a merry, laughing married woman— and arrived at Versailles a widow. Gustave, the husband whose love she would never know, perished at an early hour on the morning of her arrival, at an adversary's sword-point behind a potting-shed near the Petit Trianon. Rumour whispered that it was on account of a woman that he fought and lost, but this last blow of Providence's hatchet was spared his girl bride, innocent, secure in her supreme purity and innate virginity. If evil tongues had even mentioned the word " woman " to her, she would not have known what they meant.

Gradually the pain of her loss grew less. She commenced to enter into Court life with a certain

[1] Nicholas Ben-Hepple declares that he married her solely on account of her " dot " !

amount of zest. Ben-Hepple tells us that it was during a masked carnival in the Park of Versailles that she first attracted the attention of the amorous King. He had dropped behind Dubarry for a moment to tie up his bootlace, and Julie, running girlishly along the moonlit path, bumped violently into his arched back. With a muttered exclamation he straightened himself and tore off her mask. Ben-Hepple goes on to say that his Majesty went from scarlet to white, from white to green, and then back again to scarlet before he made his world-famed remark, " *Mon Dieu! Quelle visage!* " At this moment Dubarry appeared, furious at being left, and dragged her royal paramour away. But the mischief was done. The wheel of circumstance had turned once more—and a few days later Julie changed her *appartements* for some on a higher landing.

What vice! What intrigue! What corruption! Versailles seemed but a vast conservatory sheltering the vile soil from which sprang the lilies of France— La Belle France, as Edgar Sheepmeadow so eloquently puts it. Did any single bloom escape the blight of ineffable depravity? No—not one!

A WITHERED NOSEGAY

Occasionally some fresh young thing would appear at Court—appealing and innocent. Then the atmosphere would begin to take effect : some one would whisper something to her—she would leer almost unconsciously ; a few days later she would be discovered carrying on anyhow !

Julie de Poopinac, beautiful, accomplished and incredibly witty, queened it in this *mêlée* of appalling degeneracy ; she was not at heart wicked, but her environment closed in upon her pinched and wasted heart, crushing the youth and sweetness from it.

She held between her slim fingers the reins of government, and womanlike she twisted them this way and that, her foolish head slightly turned by adulation and flattery. Louis adored her : he gave her a cameo brooch, a beaded footstool (which his mother had used), and the loveliest cock linnet, which used to fly about all over the place, singing songs of its own composition.

All the world knows of her celebrated scene with Marie Antoinette, but Edgar Sheepmeadow recounts it so deliciously in volume III of " Women Large and Women Small " that it would be a sin not to quote it. "They met," he says, "on the Grand Staircase. The Dauphine, with her usual hauteur, was mounting with her head held high. Julie, by some misfortune, happened to get in her way. The Dauphine, not seeing her, trod heavily on her foot, then jogged her in the ribs with her elbow. Though realising who it was, the great lady could not but apologise. Drawing herself up as high as possible, she said in icy tones, ' I beg your pardon ! ' Quick as thought Julie replied, ' Granted as soon as asked ! ' Then with a toss of her curls, she ran down the stairs, leaving the haughty Princess's mind a vortex of tumultuous feelings."

A few words of description should undoubtedly be vouchsafed to the decoration of her apartments at Versailles. Artistic from birth, Julie de Poopinac inaugurated almost a revolution in colour schemes : her *salle des populaces* (room of the people), where she received supplicants for alms and various other favours, was upholstered in Godstone blue, with hangings of griffin pink ; her *salle à manger* (dining-room) was a tasteful *mélange* of elephant green, cerise, and burnt umber. Her *salle de bains* (bathroom) deserves special mention, owing to its bizarre mixture of mustard colour and veitch purple—while her *chambre à coucher* (bedroom) was a truly fitting setting for so brilliant a gem. The walls were lined with costly Bridgeport tapestries in brown and black, picked out here and there with beads and tufts of gloriously coloured wool. The bed curtains were of a soft Norwegian yellow, with massive tassels of crab mauve, while the carpet and upholstery were almost entirely Spanish crimson with headrests of Liverpool plush ! It was here, of course, that she wrote most of her poems.[1] Her world-renowned " Idyll to Summer " :—

> " Dawn,
> The poplars droop and sway and droop,
> A lazy bee
> With wings athread with gold and green·
> His merry way with ecstasy
> He takes, amid the garden blooms—
> Ah me, ah God, ah God, ah me !
> Dawn . . ."

And the perfectly delicious light poem dedicated to Louis—

[1] The extracts here quoted translated by Elizabeth Bottle.

" Beloved, it is morn—I rise
  To smell the roses sweet ;
Emphatic are my hips and thighs,
  Phlegmatic are my feet.
Ten thousand roses have I got
  Within a garden small,
Give me but strength to smell the lot,
  Oh, let me sniff them all ! "

Then her rather sordid realistic poem to Louis's deathbed commencing

" Oh, Bed
Wherein he frequently disposed
His weary limbs when day was done,
His last long sleep has murmured down—
Oh Bed—beneath your silken pall,
His eyes aglaze with death, and dim
With age—are closed.
  Oh, Bed ! "

It was of course after Louis's death that Julie was forced to seek retirement in her chateau in Old Brittany. There for many years she lived in almost complete seclusion, writing her books which were the inspired outpourings of a tortured soul : " Lilith : the Story of a Woman " ; " The Hopeless Quest," an allegorical tale of the St. Malo sand-dunes, then unexplored ; and " The Pig-Sty," a biting satire on life at Court.

Then the storm-cloud of the revolution broke athwart the length and breadth of fair France, relentless, indomitable and irredeemable. Julie was arrested while blackberrying in a Dolly Varden hat. With a brave smile, Ben-Hepple tells us, she flung the berries away. " I am ready ! " she said.

You all know of her journey to Paris, and her mockery of a trial before the tribunal—her pitiful bravery when the inhuman monsters tried to make her say " *À la lanterne !* " Nothing would induce her to—she had the firmness of many ancestors behind her.

We will quote Ben-Hepple's vivid description of her execution :—

" The day dawned grey with heavy clouds to the east," he says. " About five minutes past ten, a few rain-drops fell. The tumbrils were already rattling along amidst the frenzied jeers of the crowd. The first one contained a group of *ci-devant* aristos, laughing and singing—one elderly vicomtesse was playing on a mouth-organ. In the second tumbril sat two women—one, Marie Topinambour, a poor dancer, was weeping; the other, Julie de Poopinac, was playing at cat's cradles. Her dress was of sprigged muslin, and she wore a rather battered Dolly Varden hat. She was haughtily impervious to the vile epithets of this mob. Upon reaching the guillotine, Marie Topinambour became panic-stricken, and swarmed up one of the posts before any one could stop her. In bell-like tones, Julie bade her descend. 'Fear nothing, *ma petite*,' she cried. 'See, I am smiling!' The terrified Marie looked down and was at once calmed. Julie was indeed smiling. One or two marquises who were waiting their turn were in hysterics. Marie slowly descended, and was quickly executed. Then Julie stepped forward. '*Vive le Roi!*' she cried, for-getting in her excitement that he was already dead, and flinging her Dolly Varden hat in the very teeth of the crowd, she laid her head in the prescribed notch. A woman in the mob said '*Pauvre*' and somebody else said '*A bas!*' The knife fell. . . .''

THE DUCHESS OF WAPPING

(MADCAP MOLL)

THE DUCHESS OF WAPPING

From the world-famous portrait by Sir Oswald Cronk, Bart.

THE DUCHESS OF WAPPING
(MADCAP MOLL)

NOBODY who knew George I. could help loving him—he possessed that peculiar charm of manner which had the effect of subjugating all who came near him into immediate slavery. Madcap Moll— his true love, his one love (England still resounds with her gay laugh)—adored him with such devotion as falls to the lot of few men, be they kings or beggars.

They met first in the New Forest, where Norman Bramp informs us, in his celebrated hunting memoirs " Up and Away," the radiant Juniper spent her wild, unfettered childhood. She was ever a care-free, undisciplined creature, snapping her shapely fingers at bad weather, and riding for preference without a saddle—as hoydenish a girl as one could encounter on a day's march. Her auburn ringlets ablow in the autumn wind, her cheeks whipped to a flush by the breeze's caress, and her eyes sparkling and brimful of tomboyish mischief and roguery ! This, then, was the picture that must have met the King's gaze as he rode with a few trusty friends through the forest for his annual week of otter shooting. Upon seeing him, Madcap Moll gave a merry laugh, and crying " Chase me, George ! " in provocative tones, she rode swiftly away on her pony. Many of the courtiers trembled at such a daring exhibition of *lèse majesté*, but the King, provoked only by her winning smile, tossed his gun to Lord Twirp and set off in hot pursuit. Eventually he caught his roguish quarry by the banks of a sunlit pool. She had flung herself off her mount and flung herself on the trunk of a tree, which she bestrode as though it were a better and more fiery steed. The King cast an appraising glance at her shapely legs, and then tethered his horse to an old oak.

" Are you a creature of the woods ? " he said.

Madcap Moll tossed her curls. " Ask me ! " she cried derisively.

" I am asking you," replied the King.

" Odds fudge—you have spindleshanks ! " cried Madcap Moll irrelevantly. The King was charmed. He leant towards her.

" One kiss, mistress ! " he implored. At that she slapped his face and made his nose bleed. He was captivated.

" I'faith, art a daring girl," he cried delightedly. " Knowst who I am ? "

" I care not ! " replied the girl.

" George the First ! " said the King, rising. Madcap Moll blanched.

" Sire," she murmured, " I did not know—a poor, unwitting country lass—have mercy ! "

The King touched her lightly on the nape.

" Get up," he said gently ; " you are as loyal and spirited a girl as one could meet in all Hampshire, I'll warrant. Hast a liking for Court ? "

" Oh, sire ! " answered the girl.

Thus did the King meet her who was to mean everything in his life, and more. . . .

It was twilight in the forest, Raymond Waffle tells us, when the King rode away. In the opposite direction rode a pensive girl, her eyes aglow with something deeper than had ever before illumined their translucency.

Budde Towers, according to Plabbin's " Guide to

Hampshire," lay in the heart of the forest. Built in the days of William the Conqueror, 1066, and William Rufus, 1087, by Sir Francis Budde, it had been inhabited by none but Buddes of each successive generation. Madcap Moll's great-grandfather, Lord Edmunde Budde,[1] added a tower here and there when he felt inclined, while her uncle Robert Budde —known from Bournemouth to Lyndhurst as Bounding Bob—built the celebrated picture gallery (which can be viewed to this day by genealogical enthusiasts), the family portraits up to then having been stored in the box-room.

Old Earl Budde, Moll's father, was as crusty an old curmudgeon as one could find in a county. His wife (the lovely Evelyn Wormgate, daughter of the Duke of Bognor and Wormgate) had died while the radiant Moll was but a puling infant. Thus it was that, knowing no hand of motherly authority, the child perforce ran wild throughout her dazzling adolescence.

The trees were her playmates, the twittering of

[1] Lord Edmunde Budde married the notorious Gertrude Pippin : see " Family Failings," by Bloody Mary.

the birds her music—all the wild things of the forest loved her, specially dogs and children. She knew every woodcutter for miles round by his Christian name. " Why, here's Madcap Moll ! " they would say, as the beautiful girl came galloping athwart her mustang, untamed and headstrong as she herself.

This, then, was the priceless jewel which George I., spurred on by an overmastering passion, ordered to be transferred from its rough and homely setting to the ornate luxury of life at Court, where he immediately bestowed upon her the title of Eighth Duchess of Wapping.

It was about a month after her arrival in London that Sir Oswald Cronk painted his celebrated life-size portrait of her in the costly riding-habit which was one of the many gifts of her royal lover. Sir Oswald, with his amazing technique, has managed to convey that suggestion of determination and resolution, one might almost say obstinacy, lying behind the gay, devil-may-care roguishness of her bewitching glance. Her slim girlish figure he has portrayed with amazing accuracy, also the beautiful negligent manner in which she invariably carried her hunting-crop ; her left hand is lovingly caressing the head of her faithful hound, Roger, who, Raymond Waffle informs us, after his mistress's death refused to bury bones anywhere else but on her grave. Ah me ! Would that some of our human friends were as unflagging in their affections as the faithful Roger !

Her reign as morganatic queen was remarkable for several scientific inventions of great utility [1]— notably the " pushfast," a machine designed exclusively for the fixing of leather buttons in church hassocks ; also Dr. Snaggletooth's cunning device for separating the rind from Camembert cheese without messing the hands ! There were in addition to the examples here quoted many minor inventions which, though perhaps not of any individually intrinsic value, went far to illustrate Madcap Moll's influence on the progress of the civilisation of her time.

In Raymond Waffle's rather long-winded record of her life he dwells for several chapters upon the

[1] See Norman Bramp's " Female Influence, and Why," vol. v.

THE DUCHESS OF WAPPING

Papist plots which menaced her position at Court. After a visit to several of London's museums I have discovered that most of the facts he quotes are naught but fallacies. There were undoubtedly plots, but nothing in the least Papist. She had her enemies—who has not ? But, as far as religion was concerned, Papists, Protestants, Wesleyans, and occasionally Mahommedans, all joined together in unstinting praise of her character and judgment.

Any faults or acts of thoughtlessness committed during her brilliant life were amply compensated for by the supreme deed of loyalty and patriotism which, alas ! marked the tragic close of her all too short career. Her ride to Norwich—show me the man whose pulses do not thrill at the mention of that heroic achievement ! That wonderful, wonderful ride—that amazing, glorious *tour de force* which caused her name to be revered and hallowed in every sleepy hamlet and hovel of Old England—her ride to Norwich on Piebald Polly, her thoroughbred mare ! On, on through the night—a fitful moon scrambling aslant the cloud-blown heavens, the wind whistling past her ears, and the tune of " God Save

the King " ringing in her brain, the rhythm set by
the convulsive movements of Piebald Polly. On,
on, through towns and villages, and then once more
the open country—what is that noise ? The roaring
of water ! Torrents are unloosed—the dam has
burst ! Miller's Leap. Can she do it ?—can she ?
—can she ? She can—and has. Dawn shows in
the eastern sky—the lights of Norwich—Norwich
at last ! [1]

Poor Moll ! the day that dawned as she sped
along those weary roads was to prove itself her last.
Her exhaustion was so great on reaching the city
gates that she fell from Piebald Polly's drooping
back and never regained consciousness.

Rumour asserts that the King plunged the country
in mourning for several weeks—some say he never
smiled again. Madcap Moll, Eighth Duchess of
Wapping, left behind her no children, but she left
engraved upon the hearts of all who knew her the
memory of a beautiful, noble, and winsome woman.

---

[1] It has never yet been ascertained exactly why Madcap
Moll rode to Norwich, but many conjectures have been
hazarded.

BIANCA DI PIANNO-FORTTI

After an engraving by Vittorio Campanele

BIANCA DI PIANNO-FORTI

MEDIÆVAL Italy has in its time boasted many beautiful women, but there is one who must take her place before them all, one whose name is a byword to this day in every corner of that sun-washed country—Bianca di Pianno-Forti. One shudders at that name—so radiant was she, and yet so incredibly evil. Her tragic death somehow seems a fitting ending to a life such as hers—a life so without mercy, so without pity, and yet so amazingly vivid that it seems to be emblazoned on to Italy's very heart.

She first saw the light in Florence. Her father, Allegro, of the celebrated house of Andante Caprioso, married at the age of fourteen Giulia Presto, of Verona, at the age of nine. At the birth of Bianca her mother died, leaving her to the care of her broken-hearted father and brother Pizzicato (destined later on to make the world ring with his music). Perhaps the only thing to be said in excuse of Bianca's later conduct is the fact that she never knew a mother's love. The nuns at the convent wherein she spent her ripening childhood were kind; but, alas! they were not mothers—at least, not all of them. Bianca left the convent when she was sixteen. Slim, lissom, sinuous, with those arresting eyes that seemed, so Fibinio tells us, to search out the very souls of all who came near her. Her first love affair occurred about a week after her arrival in her home in Florence. She was in the habit of walking to mass at the cathedral with her maid Vivace. One morning, so Poliolioli relates, a handsome soldier stepped out of the shadows of an adjoining buttress and looked at her. Bianca at once swooned. The same thing happened again—and again—and yet again. One night she heard the shutters of her bed-chamber rattle! "Who is there?" she cried, yet not too loudly, because her woman's instinct warned her to be wary. The shutters were flung open, and the young soldier stepped flamboyantly into the room. "I am here, *cara, cara mia!*" he cried. "I, Vibrato Adagio!" With a sibilant cry she fell into his outstretched arms. "*Mio, mio*," she echoed in ecstasy, " I am yours and you are mine ! " So lightly was the first stepping-stone passed on her reckless path of immorality and vice. Her fickle heart soon tired of the debonair Vibrato, and in a fit of satiated pique she had his ears cut off and his tongue removed and tied to his big toe. Thus was her ever-increasing lust for bloodshed apparent even at that early age. Her next *affaire* occurred when she was travelling to Rome with her brother Pizzi-cato, who was to become a chorister at the Vatican. On stopping for refreshment at a wayside tavern, Bianca was struck by the arresting looks of the ostler who was tending their steaming steeds. Beckoning to him, she asked of him his name ; he turned his vacant eyes round and round wonderingly for a moment. " Crescendo," he replied. Bianca's eyes flashed fire. " *Accelerato !* " she cried imperiously, and, hypnotised into submission, the scared man fled upstairs, Bianca following.

Upon arriving in Rome, Bianca and Pizzicato repaired to their father's brother-in-law, who was well known as a lavish entertainer. He was one Rapidamente Tempo di Valse, a widower, living with his two sons, Lento and Comprino—handsome lads both in the first flush of manhood, and both destined to fall victims to Bianca's compelling attractions. Contemporary history informs us that Bianca stayed in the Palazzo Tempo di Valse for seven years, visiting Pizzicato from time to time, and employing herself with various love affairs.

In June she became betrothed to Duke Crazioso di Pianno-Forti, of the famous family of Moderato e Diminuendo—indirectly descended from the Cardinal Appassionato Tutti. Tutti was the great-uncle of the infamous Con Spirito, well known to posterity as the lover of the lovely but passionate Violenza Allargando, destined to become the mother of Largo con Craviata, the fearless captain of Dolcissimo's light horse under General Lamento Agitato, whose grandmother, Sempre Calando, was notorious for her illicit liaison with Pesante e Stentato, a union which was to bear fruit in the shape of Lusingando Molto.

Bianca's wedding was celebrated with enormous rejoicing in Venice, where was situated the ducal palace of the Pianno-Fortis. Mention should be made of the life led by Bianca during the first years of her marriage, of her pet staghounds, of her tapestried bedchamber with bloodthirsty scenes of the chase depicted thereon—how she loved blood, this beautiful girl !

Her portrait herein reproduced is after an engraving by Campanele ; note the sinister line of the cheek-bone and the passionate beauty of the nethermost lip ! One can visualise her—radiant at the head of crowded dining-tables, drinking from gem-encrusted goblets, accepting glances fraught with ardent desire from one or other of the male guests.

All the world knows of her famous visit to the Pope, and how he died a few hours later ; while it would be mere repetition of general knowledge to enlarge on her sojourn with the Doge, and his subsequent demise. Let us touch ever so lightly on her three children, Poco, Confuoco, and Strepi-toso. How could they help being beautiful with such a mother, poor mites, branded from birth with the sense of their impending fate ! After a while Bianca became aware that tongues were a-wag in Venice, sullying her name with foul calumnies.

A WITHERED NOSEGAY

Her decision for their downfall was swift and terrible. She persuaded her easy-going husband to ride to Naples ; then, free of his cumbersome authority, she set to work on the preparations for her world-famous supper party. Picture it if you will : five hundred and eighty-three guests [1] all seated laughingly in the immense banqueting-hall—Bianca at the head of the table, superb, incomparable, her corsage a glittering mass of gems, her breast chilled by the countless diamonds on her camisole, her smile radiant and a peach-like flush on the ivory pallor of her face. This was indeed her hour—her triumph—her subtle revenge. Her heart thrilled with the knowledge of that inward secret that was hers immutably, for every morsel of food and drink upon that festive board was impregnated with the deadliest poison—all except the two pieces of toast with which she regaled herself, having dined earlier and alone.

Historians tell us that following close on that event some rather ugly rumours were noised abroad

[1] Poliolioli contends that there were five hundred and eighty-five guests. This, I think, may be treated as a moot point.

BIANCA DI PIANNO-FORTI

—in fact, some of the relatives of the poisoned guests even went so far as to complain to various people in authority and stir up strife in every way possible. Bianca was naturally furious. Some say that it was her sudden rage on hearing this that caused her to burn her children to death ; others say her act was merely due to bad temper owing to a sick headache. Anyhow, as later events go to show, she had chosen the very worst time to murder her children. More ugly rumours were at once noised abroad by those who were jealous of her. Upon her husband's return from Naples he was immediately arrested, and a few days later hung. Too late the hapless Bianca sought to make her escape ; she was caught and taken prisoner while swimming across the Grand Canal with her clothes and a few personal effects in a bundle in her mouth. She was carried shrieking to Milan, where she endured a mockery of a trial ; on political grounds she was sentenced to being torn to pieces by she-goats at Genoa. Poor, beautiful Bianca ! On the fulfilment of her unjust and barbarous sentence it is too horrible to dwell at any length. This glorious creature, this

resplendent vision, this divine goddess—she-goats !
Dreadful, degrading, unutterable ! ! !

The day for her death [1] dawned fair over the
Mediterranean. Bianca, garbed in white, walked
with dignity into the meadow wherein the she-goats
anxiously awaited her. She bravely repressed a
shudder, and fell upon her knees. History tells us
that every goat turned away, as though ashamed of
the part it was destined to play. Then, with a look
of ineffable peace stealing over her waxen face,
Bianca rose to her full height, and, flinging her arms
heavenwards, she delivered that celebrated and
heartrending speech which has lived after her for so
long :—

" *Dio mio, concerto—concerto !* "

One by one the she-goats advanced. . . .

---

[1] October 14th.   Poliolioli contests that it was the 17th, but
this, I venture to say, is even a " mooter " point than the other.

SARAH, LADY TUNNELL-PENGE

SARAH, LADY TUNNELL-PENGE

From a painting by Augustus Punter

SARAH, LADY TUNNELL-PENGE

FFRADDLE of 1643 was very different from the Ffraddle of 1789, and still more different from the Ffraddle of 1832. At a time when civil war was raging between Jacobites and Papists and Roundheads and Ironsides and everything, Ffraddle stood grey, silent and indomitable—the very spirit of peace allied with strength seemed embodied in its grim masonry. The clash of arms and the death cries from millions of rebellious throats which echoed athwart the length and breadth of young England were unable to pierce the stillness of Ffraddle's moated security. Owls murmured on its battered turrets, sparrows perched on its portcullis, cuckoos cooed all over it, heedless indeed of the turmoil and frenzied strife raging outside its feudal gates.

What a birthplace for one of history's most priceless pearls—Sarah Twig! The heart of every lover of beauty leaps and jumps and starts at the sound of that name—Sarah Twig. Why are some destined for so much while others are destined, alas! for so little ?—Who knows ? Sarah—a rose-leaf, a crumpled atom, dropped as it were from some heavenly garden into the black times of the Merry Monarch— when, according to Bloodworthy, virtue was laughed to scorn and evil went unpunished ; when, according to Follygob, virginity was a scream and harlotry a hobby ; and when, according to Sheepmeadow, homeliness was sin, and beauty but a gilded casket concealing vice and depravity unutterable.

History relates that though food was scarce and light hearts hard to find, at the birth of Sarah Twig there was no dearth of these commodities. The snow was on the ground, Follygob says—the woods and coppices and hills lay slumbering beneath a glistening white mantle. What a mind ! To have written those words ! It was undoubtedly Folly-gob's artistic style and phraseology that branded him once and for all as the master chronicler of his time.

Sarah Twig was born in the east wing—a lofty room which can be viewed to this day by all true lovers of historical architecture. To describe it adequately is indeed difficult. Some say there was a bed in it and an early Norman window ; others have it that there was no bed but a late Gothic fireplace ; while a few outstanding writers insist that there was nothing at all in the room but a very old Roman washstand.[1]

The night of Sarah's birth was indeed a wild one—snow and sleet eddied and swirled around the massive structure destined to harbour one whose radiant beauty was to be a byword in all Europe. The wind, so Follygob with his incomparable style tells us, lashed itself to a livid fury against the sturdy Ffraddle turrets and mullions, whilst outside beyond the keep and raised drawbridge the beacons and camp fires stained the frost-laden air with vivid streaks of red and yellow—colours which formed the background of the Ffraddle coat of arms, thus presenting an omen to the startled inhabitants which history relates they were not slow to recognise.

Bloodworthy describes for us the plan by which Lord Ffraddle was to acquaint the village with the

[1] Excavated B.C. 8.

sex of the child. If it were a boy, red fire was to be burnt on the south turret, and if a girl, green fire was to be burnt on the north turret ; but unfortunately, he goes on to tell us, owing to some misadventure blue fire was firmly burnt on all the turrets. Imagine the horror of the superstitious populace ! Some left the country never to return, crying aloud that a chameleon had been born to their beloved chatelaine !

Of Sarah's youth historians tell us little. She was, apart from her beauty, a very knowing child. Often when missing from the banqueting-hall she would be discovered in the library reading and studying the political works of the period.[1] Often Lord Ffraddle was known to remark in his usual witty way, " In sooth, the child will soon have as much knowledge as her father," a sally which was invariably received with shrieks of delight by the infant Sarah, whose brilliant sense of humour was plainly apparent, even at that early age.

[1] Periodicals :—" The Corn Chandler," by Sheepmeadow ; " Sidelights on the Salic Law," Anonymous ; " The Stage *versus* the Church," edited alternately by Nell Gwyn and the Archbishop of Canterbury.

SARAH, LADY TUNNELL-PENGE

Her adolescence was remarkable for little save the rapid development of her supple loveliness, some idea of which can be gauged from the reproduction of Punter's famous portrait on page 46. Though painted at a somewhat later date, this masterpiece still presents us with most of the leading characteristics of its ravishing model. Note the eyes—the dreamy, cognisant expression ; glance at the pretty mouth and the dainty ears. Her demeanour is obviously that of a meek and modest woman, but Punter, with his true genius, has caught that glint of inward fire, that fleeting look of shy mischief that earned for her the world-famous nickname of " Winsome Sal."

It was when she was eighteen [1] that Destiny, with inhuman cunning, caught up in his net the fragile ball of her life.

The handsome, devil-may-care Julius Fenchurch-Streete applied to Lord Ffraddle for a secretary-ship, which was ultimately granted to him. Imagine the situation—this rake, this dark-eyed ne'er-do-well, notorious all down Cheapside for his relentless

[1] Two years before Punter's portrait.

dalliance with the fair, placed in intimate proximity with one of England's most glorious specimens of ripening womanhood. It was, Sheepmeadow writes, like the meeting of flint and tinder—these two so widely different in the essentials and yet so akin in their physical beauty. As was inevitable, from the first they loved—he with the flaming passion of a hell-rake, she with the sweet, appealing purity of one whose whole life had been peculiarly virginal. There followed swiftly upon their ardent confessions the determination to elope together. The night they bade adieu to Ffraddle and all it held is well known to young and old of every generation. They crept from their rooms at midnight and met at the top of the grand staircase, down which they proceeded to crawl on all fours. A few moments later they were on a sturdy mare, she riding pillion, he riding anyhow. Not a sound had been heard, not a dog had barked, not a bird had called. Once, Sheepmeadow informs us, Lady Ffraddle turned over in her sleep.[1] Poor, unsuspecting mother ! On and

[1] " Beds and their Inmates," vol. III., by Edgar Sheepmeadow (18 vols.).

on through the snow rode the feckless couple. Once Sarah rested her hand lightly on her lover's arm. " Whither are we bound ? " she inquired. " Only the mare knows that," Julius replied, and in shaken silence they rode on.

History is not very enlightening as to how long Julius Fenchurch-Streete lived with Sarah Twig—poor Sarah, the bubble of her romance soon was to be pricked. For three weeks they lived gloriously, radiantly, at the old sign of " The Cod and Haddock " in Egham. " My heart is a pool of ecstasy," she wrote in her diary. Pitiful pool, so soon to be drained of its joy !

Then the storm-clouds gathered—the sun withdrew its gold. Julius rode away—Sarah was alone, alone in Egham, her love unblessed by any sort of church, no name for the child to come—a sorry, sorry plight. The buxom proprietress of " The Cod and Haddock," little dreaming her real identity, set her to work. Work ! for those fair hands, those inexpressibly filbert nails !

Was it the sudden relenting of a malleable fate that caused the Merry Monarch to come riding blithely through sleepy Egham, followed by his equerry, Lord Francis Tunnell-Penge, and several of his suite ? Halting outside the inn, Bloodworthy relates that his Majesty was immediately struck by a winsome face at an upper window. " Lud ! " he cried laconically, and dismounted, taking several dogs from his hat as he did so, and one from his pocket ; for he was devoted to animals, Bloodworthy goes on to say, and often spent days stroking their soft ears abstractedly. Then, seized by a sudden inspiration, he inquired of the landlady as to whose was the face he had seen. In a trice the story was told—the King waved his hand imperiously and took a pinch of snuff. " Send her to me," he said.

When Sarah entered, all hot from her manual labours, Charles started to his feet. Here was no scullion, no plaything of an idle hour. Here was breeding, dignity and beauty. Ah ! Beauty ! Probably these cold shores will never again shelter beauty like Sarah Twig's. On seeing the King she curtsied low. He bowed with the stately elegance for which he was famed.

" Your name ? " he asked.

SARAH, LADY TUNNELL-PENGE

The glorious vision veiled her eyes.

" I have no name, sire—now." With these words, spoken from a heart surcharged with bitterest sorrow, the poor woman swooned away.

" Lud ! " remarked the King irritably, " the girl must have a name. You must marry her, Francis— she shall be Lady Tunnell-Penge." Then the impulsive monarch stooped, and, opening a locket on the unconscious woman's breast, read the name Sarah in blue diamonds on an opaque background. " But," he added softly under his breath, " I shall know her only as ' Winsome Sal ' ! "

Thus Sarah Twig, so nearly an outcast through her own girlish folly, became possessor of a name honoured and even adored throughout England.

The first few years of her life at Court were more or less uneventful—she saw little of her husband and lots of the King. He and she used to wander along the river side, simply loaded with different dogs. Whenever there were theatricals given Sheepmeadow tells us, Sarah invariably appeared as Diana or Minerva, preferring these parts on account of their suitability to her youth and figure. All these events took place long after Punter's portrait, though several others were done latterly. Her wit and gaiety were of course world-famed, and her political treatises are preserved to this day.[1]

On one dramatic occasion her brilliant political knowledge and presence of mind were the means of saving England from turmoil or worse. Hearing that the people were hungry and restless, Sarah rushed to the King. " What's to do ? " she cried breathlessly.

" God knows," replied Charles, adding " Lud ! " as an afterthought. Then he went on fondling the long silky ears of one of the lap-dogs with which the room was strewn.

Heartbroken, Sarah left the room and rushed out of Whitehall as fast as her legs could carry her, heeding not the jeers of the crowd. She made for Tower Hill, from the summit of which she delivered her world-famed political speech, ending with the stirring words, " Sift your corn through sieves ! "

How that speech sends a throb to one's heart— the defiance of it, the subtlety of it, and yet the intense

[1] These are all in the Brighton Aquarium.

womanliness of it ! The people cheered her back to the Palace. She went straight to the King's room— he was feeding his dogs.

" I've saved England ! " cried Sarah exultantly.

" Lud ! " replied the King, and handed her some cat's-meat. No wonder women loved him !

Incidents like these went to make up the multi-coloured mosaic of Sarah, Lady Tunnell-Penge's life. Her children were many—Arthur, later on Lord Crumpingfax ; Muriel, later the Duchess of Dripp ; and various others.

She died at the age of seventy-nine,[1] thus out-living her Royal paramour. A beautiful life, a noble life, a gentle life—yet was there something missing ? Sometimes I gaze at her portrait and wonder.

[1] At Pragg Castle, near Hull.

FÜRSTIN LIEBERWURST ZU SCHWEINEN-KALBER

FURSTIN LIEBERWURST ZU SCHWEINEN-KALBER

From the famous etching by Grobmayer

FURSTIN LIEBERWURST ZU SCHWEINEN-KALBER

HOW strange it seems that she of whom we write is dust and less than dust below the fertile soil of her so beloved Prussia—Furstin Lieberwurst zu Schweinen-Kalber! Can you not rise from the grave once more to charm us with the magic of your voice? Are those deep, mellowed tones, so sonorous and appealing, never to be heard again? Ah, me! Why, indeed, should such divinity be so short lived? Who could play Juliet as she could! Nobody! Her enemies laughed and said that her chronic adenoids utterly destroyed all the beauty of the part. Jealousy! Vile jealousy! Genius always has that to contend with. Every one has failings. Gretchen Lieberwurst zu Schweinen-Kalber made of Juliet a woman—a pulsating, human woman, with failings like the rest of us, the chief of which happened to be adenoids.[1]

[1] See Sheepmeadow's " Heroines and their Diseases."

A WITHERED NOSEGAY

To trace this soul-stirring actress to her obscure birth has indeed been a labour—but withal, a labour of love! For who could help experiencing exquisite joy at unearthing trinkets and miniatures and broken memories of such a radiant being?

Nuremburg, red-roofed and gleaming in the sunlight, was the place wherein she first saw the light of day. Her father, Peter Schmidt, was by trade a sausage-moulder, for in those far-off days there was not the vast machinery of civilisation to wield the good meat into the requisite shape. Gretchen, when a girl, often used to watch her father as he plied his trade and recite to him verses she had learnt at her dame school—fragments from the Teutonic masterpieces of the time—" Kruschen Kruschen," and—

> " Baby white and baby red,
> Like a moon convulsive
> Rolling up and down the bed,
> Utterly repulsive ! "—

a beautiful little lullaby of Herman Veigel's. Gretchen used to recite it with the tears pouring down her cheeks, so poignantly affected was she by the sensitive beauty of it. Her father also used to weep hopelessly—also her mother, if she happened to be near ; and Heinrich, the cat, invariably retreated under the sofa, unutterably moved.

Life dragged on with some monotony for Gretchen. She often used to help her mother in the kitchen— and occasionally in the sitting-room. One day she became a woman ! Every one noticed it. Neighbours used to meet her mother in the *strasse* and say, " Fraulein Schmidt, your Gretchen is a woman." Fraulein Schmidt would nod proudly and reply, " Yes, we have seen that ; my Peter and I—we are very happy." Thus Gretchen left her girlhood behind her. It was her habit, so Grundelheim tells us, to walk out in the forest with one Hans Breitel, an actor at the municipal theatre. He used to teach her to talk to the birds, and when she besought him ardently to tell her stories of the theatre, he would relate to her the parts he had nearly played. Gretchen's heart thrilled—oh to be an actress, an actress ! On her twenty-fourth birthday, von Bottiburgen [1] tells us, Gretchen left home, and went

[1] Von Bottiburgen, science master at the Munich College, author and compiler of the following :—" Our Women " ; " Do Actresses Mind Much ? " ; " Life of Fritz Schnotter."

to Berlin. She wanted to get an interview with Goethe. One day, after she had been in Berlin a little while, she found him. Brampenrich describes the scene for us, so beautifully and with such truly exquisite rotundity of style :—

" The Great Goethe ate at his lunch. What was that noise ? He swiftly puts down his knife : the door bursts open ; Gretchen Schmidt enters, her lovely hair awry, her cheeks flushed. ' I will act ! ' she cries in bell-like tones. ' *Ach, ach !* ' cries Goethe. Then Gretchen, with a superb gesture, hangs her hat on the door handle, and recites to the amazed man his beloved ' Faust,' word for word, syllable for syllable ! "

Thus Brampenrich shows us, with his supreme word imagery, what really happened.

Gretchen never saw Goethe again ; he left Berlin almost immediately for the Black Forest. Gretchen, alone in the great Capital, alone and a woman, what could she do ? Grundelheim, in his celebrated " Toilers who have Toiled," relates how desperately hard she worked with her mangle in the Konig-strasse. Then one day, when things seemed at their

FURSTIN LIEBERWURST

blackest, Romance, with its multi-coloured finger, poked a hole in the bubble of her existence. The King of Prussia drove along the Konigstrasse, bowing to right and left. Gretchen stepped lightly over her mangle and dropped a curtsey. The King was immediately captivated, and a few hours later the happy girl found herself in the Royal Palace. After that events moved rapidly. At the lax German Court Gretchen soon forgot her austere upbringing, and entered into the round games and charades with untold abandon! Alas! the fickle heart of the King was soon turned from her. Realising this, Gretchen seized upon a noble much enamoured of her, Furst Lieberwurst zu Schweinen-Kalber, and married him one spring morning in the Chapel Royal. For three months they lived together in the Austrian Tyrol; then Gretchen, heeding at last the persistent call of her art, left him, and fled back to Berlin, where she obtained an engagement to play Juliet. It was from that moment that her real passion for her part developed. It grew to be an obsession—she was fêted, lauded, mentioned in several public speeches. For sixty-five years she played it all over Germany, never tiring, never weakening. People gibbered over her ; then came her tragic death at the age of ninety-two in the balcony scene. She stumbled forwards, Grundelheim says, then backwards, then forwards, then backwards again, and then forwards for the last time. The balcony gave way, and she fell at Romeo's feet (it was the great Fritz Schnotter, with whom she had been playing for two years : in private life he was, of course, her lover—she always insisted on that).

History tells us that he caught her in his arms— Bottiburgen contests that he caught her in the middle of his chest ; anyhow, the house is said to have risen and cheered, thinking it was a new scene suddenly interpolated. Then the curtain slowly fell, and they realised the truth—they would never see their idolised Gretchen again.

In passing, it would perhaps be as well to mention some of the famous Romeos who played opposite this bewitcher of all sexes. There was Reginald Bug, a young Englishman, who loved her passionately for a few years ; then the renowned Pierre Dentifrice from the Comédie Francaise ; then Angelo Carlini, and Basto Caballero (founder of the Shakespearean Theatre in Barcelona) ; then Dimitri Chuggski, a very temperamental, highly strung Russian (it is in volume VIII. of Edgar Sheepmeadow's " Beds and their Inmates " that he relates the story of Chuggski's desertion of Gretchen ; he contends that he left her because she always slept with her mouth open).

Her last and most famous lover on and off the stage was the aforementioned Fritz Schnotter ; he is treated lavishly in three volumes of Bottiburgen.

Her portrait on page 60 is a reproduction of Grobmayer's etching. The original could formerly be viewed, I believe, by applying to the Kaiser for permission and paying 18,000 marks.

DONNA ISABELLA ANGELICA Y BANANAS

DONNA ISABELLA ANGELICA Y BANANAS

From the portrait by Baloona (early Spanish)

DONNA ISABELLA ANGELICA Y BANANAS

SPAIN has ever been the home of romance and beauty and fiery passion, but never in its whole history has it bred such a tremulously beautiful love story as that of Donna Isabella Angelica y Bananas. A romance of two passionate hearts in such a vivid setting cannot but fail to make the eye kindle and the pulses throb. Compared to it, Lancelot and Elaine become cardboard puppets, Dante and Beatrice figures of clay utterly devoid of life, while Paolo and Francesca appear merely idiotic.

Picture to yourself, if you will, the Spain of the Middle Ages ; if you can't, it doesn't matter. Isabella Angelica was born at Seville in 1582, the daughter of Don Juan de Cabarajal and Maria his wife. Don Juan owned the Castello del Hurtado, having been left it by his infamous but regal uncle, Don Lopez a Basastos.

The Castello lay surrounded in the foreground by

turrets and moats, in the middle distance by orange groves and extraordinarily verdant meadows ; while in the background the majestic Pyrenees, rearing their snowy peaks in serried ranks of symmetrical splendour, imparted to the whole thing the semblance of rugged grandeur which is the birthright of every true Spaniard. Isabella Angelica's childhood dawned and waned in these exquisite surroundings : she would play with her tutors various games, some of them traditional, such as " catch orange " and " *raralara*," [1] and now and then frolics of her own invention, for history tells us she was ever a merry little trickster. It was not until she was seventeen that the true radiance of her beauty became apparent. Her mother had been wiser to guard the child more closely than she did, for do we not read in Dr. Polata's " From Girl to Woman " that between the ages of nineteen and twenty she was constantly seen mounting the Pyrenees in a daring fashion and entirely unattended ? But still, doubtless owing to her charming nature, which was a sweet composition of mischief and kindliness, she remained un-

[1] Spanish equivalent to " tag " or " he."

spoilt by this undesirable contact with a rude world which should, until her marriage, have been outside her girlish ken.

When she reached the age of twenty—" the very threshold of womanhood," as Fernando Lope so beautifully puts it—she was betrothed to Pedro y Bananas, a noble fresh from the vice and debauchery of the Court at Valladolid. Knowing naught of love or passion, she consented without hesitation, being but a tool in the hands of her parents, and a few months later the wedding took place with enormous pomp in the Cathedral at Seville.

After the ceremony the bride and bridegroom repaired to the Palazza Bananas, the country seat of Pedro, who, though poor himself, had had many costly estates handed down to him.

Here, so report tells us, after subjugating Isabella Angelica for three years to the vilest insults and utmost cruelty, Pedro left her temporarily and returned to the Court, now at Castille. Poor Isabella Angelica ! This was the gay world she had dreamed of—the ecstatic life she had hoped and fully expected to live !

A WITHERED NOSEGAY

Then suddenly, with the departure of her husband, she found peace—peace in the rocky solitudes, in the scented gardens and rolling foothills ; and here this poor, lonely woman found fulfilment of all her maiden dreams—" Love ! "

No one knows the authentic story of her first meeting with Enrique Baloona. Some say he was fishing for *bolawallas* [1] and she came graciously up and asked him the time ; others aver that he was passing beneath her lattice and she dropped a fluted hair-tidy at his feet. But anyhow, from the time they first met they never parted until it was absolutely necessary. They pursued the course of their love through the long, tranquil summer days and nights—every word they uttered one to the other was sheer poetry. Enrique, who was a fully qualified academician, painted the portrait reproduced on page 70. It is, alas ! the only one in existence, all the others having been destroyed by the Inquisition.

But alack ! as is the way with all beauty, it is but short-lived. The end of their peaceful passion came with the announcement of Pedro's return from the

[1] *Bolawalla*—Spanish equivalent for "mullet."

Court, now at Aragon. Isabella Angelica, history relates, was beside herself with misery. Enrique also was considerably upset. Together the doomed couple arranged a plan of escape. They flew together to the Villa Morla, a notorious abode of illicit lovers. It was here that the enraged Pedro caught up with them and killed Enrique with a look. Isabella Angelica was then taken against her will to join the Court. At last at Madrid. For two years, Dr. Polata tells us, her heart was numb with anguish ; then gradually the life at Court, still at Madrid, began to take effect on her malleable character. She became intensely vicious : much of the sweetness portrayed in Enrique's portrait vanished, leaving her expression cross and occasionally even sullen. All the world knows of her meeting with the Infanta, so we will not dwell upon it. One day her husband died unexpectedly. Cruel-minded courtiers suspected Isabella Angelica, but she was so obviously crushed that their suspicions were allayed. Her heart exulted—she had killed him with a poisoned pen-wiper. No one knew. Poor Isabella Angelica ! Her tragic love affair had indeed transformed her from the appealing girl of yesterday to the recklessly unhappy woman of to-day, forced on to the path of cruelty and vice by unlooked-for circumstances. She performed this deed and that with almost mechanical diabolicism ; some say she knew not one day from another. In 1597 she was offered an exceedingly good position by the Inquisition, which she immediately accepted. It was, she felt, her only chance of happiness—to have the opportunity of inventing a few good tortures would comfort her ; and why not ? People of to-day, narrow and unsympathetic, may censure her as being spiteful and unkind, but in those days things were—oh, so different !

She sent for her little brother and had him burnt ; this eased the pain at her heart a little. Then her aunt was conveyed to her from Majorca, and on arrival was pierced by several bodkins and ultimately buried in hot tar. Isabella Angelica almost gave vent to a wan smile.

She supervised her father's death, the actual work being performed by her colleagues of the Inquisition. He was cut in moderate-sized snippets and toasted on one side only.

DONNA ISABELLA

It says much for Isabella Angelica's charm and personality that the populace, in spite of their knowledge of her deeds, one and all adored her—to the end of her life the unstinting love and adulation of all who came in contact with her was hers irretrievably.

It was during the personal mutilation of her third cousin that she caught the influenza cold which cost her her life. Poor, doomed Isabella Angelica : her deathbed was surrounded by heart-broken mourners who had flocked from all parts of sunny Spain to pay tribute to the dying beauty ; the Inquisition issued an edict that no eyes were to be put out for a whole week in honour of her.

She died peacefully, clasping an ivory rosary and a faded miniature on elephant's hide, portraying a handsome, debonair young man. Could it have been Enrique Baloona ?

Thus lived and died one of Spain's most entrancing specimens of feminine beauty.

MAGGIE McWHISTLE

MAGGIE McWHISTLE

From an old painting by Ronald Gerphipps

MAGGIE McWHISTLE

BORN in an obscure Scotch manse of Jacobite parents, Maggie McWhistle goes down to immortality as perhaps the greatest heroine of Scottish history; and perhaps not. We read of her austere Gallic beauty in every record and tome of the period— one of the noble women whose paths were lit for them from birth by Destiny's relentless lamp. What did Maggie know of the part she was to play in the history of her country? Nothing. She lived through her girlhood unheeding; she helped her mother with the baps and her father with the haggis; occasionally she would be given a new plaidie—she who might have had baps, haggis, and plaidies ten thousandfold for the asking. A word must be said of her parents. Her father, Jaimie, known all along Deeside as Handsome Jaimie—how the light-hearted village girls mourned when he turned minister: he was high, high above them. Of his meeting with Janey McToddle, the Pride of Bonny Donside, very little is written. Some say that they met in a snow-storm on Ben Lomond, where she was tending her kine ; others say that they met on the high road to Aberdeen and his collie Jeannie bit her collie Jock— thus cementing a friendship that was later on to ripen into more and more—and even Maggie. Some years later they were wed, and Jaimie led his girl-bride to the little manse which was destined to be the birthplace of one of Scotland's saviours. History tells us little of Maggie McWhistle's child-hood : she apparently lived and breathed like any more ordinary girl—her girdle cakes were famous adown the length and breadth of Aberdeen. Gradu-ally a little path came to be worn between the manse and the kirk, seven miles away, where Maggie's feet so often trod their way to their devotions. She was intensely religious.

One day a stranger came to Aberdeen. He had braw, braw red knees and bonnie, bonnie red hair. History tells us that on first seeing Maggie in her plaidie he smiled, and that the second time he saw her he guffawed, so light-hearted was he.

One day he called at the manse, chucked Maggie

under the chin, and ate one of her baps. Eight years later he came again, and, after tweaking her nose, ate a little haggis. By then something seemed to have told her that he was her hero.

One dark night, so the story runs, there came a hammering on the door. Maggie leapt out of her truckle, and wrapping her plaidie round her, for she was a modest girl, she ran to the window.

" Wha is there ? " she cried in Scotch.

The answer came back through the darkness, thrilling her to the marrow :

" Bonnie Prince Charlie ! "

Maggie gave a cry, and, running downstairs, opened the door and let him in. She looked at him in the light shed by her homely candle. His brow was amuck with sweat : he was trembling in every limb ; his ears were scarlet.

" What has happened ? "

" I am pursued," he replied, hoarse with exertion and weariness. " Hide me, bonnie lassie, hide me, hide me ! "

Quick as thought, Maggie hid him behind the

door, and not a moment too soon. Then she displayed that strength of will and courage which was to stamp her as a heroine for all time. There came a fresh hammering on the door. Maggie opened it defiantly, and never flinched at the sight of so many brawny men; she only wrapped her plaidie more tightly round her.

" We want Bonnie Prince Charlie," said the leader, in Scotch.

Then came Maggie's well-known answer, also in Scotch.

" Know you not that this is a manse ? "

History has it that the man fell back as though struck, and one by one, awed by the still purity of the white-faced girl, the legions departed into the night whence they had come. Thus Maggie McWhistle proved herself the saviour of Bonnie Prince Charlie for the first time.

There were many occasions after that in which she was able to prove herself a heroine for his sake. She would conceal him up the chimney or in the oven at the slightest provocation. Soon there were no trees for thirty miles round in which she had not hidden him at some period or another.[1]

Poor Maggie—perchance she is finding in heaven the peaceful rest which was so lacking in her life on earth. For legend hath it that she never had two consecutive nights' sleep for fifteen years, so busy was she saving Bonnie Prince Charlie.

Then came that great deed which even now finds an exultant echo in the heart of every true Scotsman—that deed which none but a bonnie, hardy Highland lassie could have got away with. . . . You all know of the massing of James's troops at Carlisle, and later at Glasgow, and later still at Aberdeen. Poor Prince Charlie—so sonsie and braw, a fugitive in his own land—he fled to Loch Morich, followed by Maggie McWhistle in her plaidie, carrying some haggis and baps to comfort him in his exile. History is rather hazy as to exactly what happened ; but anyhow, Maggie, with the tattered banner of her country fast unfurling in her heart, decided to save her hero for the last time ; and it

---

[1] Bloodworthy says : " It was her fond boast that she never hid him in the same tree twice."

was well she did not tarry longer, for he was sore pressed. History relates that two tears fell from his eyes on to the shore.[1] Then Maggie, with a brave smile, handed him a bap.

" Eat," she said in Scotch ; " you are probably very hungry."

These simple words, spoken straight from her heart, had the effect, so chroniclers inform us, of pulling him together a bit.

" Where can I hide ? " he asked.

Maggie looked at him fearlessly for a moment.

" You shall hide in a tree," she cried, with sudden inspiration.

Bonnie Prince Charlie fell on his braw red knees.

" Please, " he cried pleadingly, " could it be an elm ? I'm so tired of gnarled oaks."

" Yes ! " cried the courageous girl exultantly. ' Quick, we will trick them yet."

Then came the supreme moment—the act of sheer devotion that was to brand that simple soul

---

[1] Bloodworthy, in telling the story, says that only one tear fell ; but Bloodworthy, brilliant recorder as he was, was occasionally prejudiced.

through the ages as a noble martyr in, alas! a lost cause. Shading her eyes with her hand, she perceived a legion of the enemy encamped on the one island of which the lonely Gallic loch boasted. Her woman's wit had devised a plan. Flinging baps and haggis to the winds, she leapt into a boat and began to row—you all know the story of that fateful row. Round and round the island she went for three weeks,[1] never heeding her tired arms and weary hands; blisters came and went, but she felt them not; her hat flew off, but the lion-hearted woman never stopped;[2] and all to convince the troops on the island that it was a fleet approaching under the command of Bonnie Prince Charlie. Completely routed, every officer and man swum to the mainland and beat a retreat, and not until the last of them had gone did Maggie relinquish her hold on the creaking oars.

[1] The reproduction on page 80 from the celebrated picture by Gerphipps—in oils at the National Gallery, in water colour at the Tate Gallery, and in Paripan at the Edinburgh Art Museum.

[2] The picture represents Maggie at the end of the second week.

A WITHERED NOSEGAY

Thus did the strategy of a simple Highland lassie defeat the aims of generals whose hearts and souls had been steeped from birth in the sanguinary ways of war. Of her journey home with the Prince you all know; and what her white-haired father said when she arrived you've heard hundreds of times. There has been a lot of argument as to the exact form the Prince's gratitude took. Some say he unwrapped her plaidie and went away with it; others write that he cut a lock of his braw red hair and gave it to her with his usual merry smile; but the authentic version of that moving scene is that of the burnt scone. Maggie had baked a scone and handed it to him; then, after he had bitten it, he handed it back.

" Nay, lassie, nay," he is said to have remarked. " My purse is empty but my heart is full. Take this scone imprinted by my royal teeth, and treasure it."

Then with a debonair bow and a ready laugh, a mocking shout and a whimsical wink, he went out into dreary Galway—a homeless wanderer.

Of Maggie's death very little is known. Some say

MAGGIE McWHISTLE

she died of hay-fever ; others say it was nasal catarrh ; but only her old mother, with a woman's unerring instinct, guessed the truth : in reality she died of a broken heart and a burnt scone.

ANNA PODD

ANNA PODD

From a very old Russian oleograph

ANNA PODD

THOUGH of humble origin, though poor and unblessed with any of life's luxuries, Anna Podd made her way in the world with unfaltering determination. The tragedy of her life was perhaps her ambition, but who could blame her for wishing to better herself? She had nothing—nothing but her beauty. What a woman's beauty can do for herself and her country is amply portrayed in the kaleidoscopic pageant of Anna Podd's life. The only existing picture of her (here reproduced) was discovered in Moscow after Ivan Buminoff's well-remembered siege, lasting seventeen years. Poor Anna! Destiny seemed ruthlessly determined to lead her so far and no farther. A Tsar loved her, which is more than falls to the lot of some women, yet fate's unrelenting finger was forever placed upon the pulse of her career.

Of her parents nothing is known. We first hear of her in a low cabaret in St. Petersburg West.

A WITHERED NOSEGAY

All night, so Serge Tadski tells us in " Russian Realism," it was her sordid duty to flaunt that exquisite loveliness which Heaven had bestowed upon her before the devouring eyes of every sort and description of Russian man. She was wont to sway rhythmically and sinuously to the crazy band which played for her ; now and then, with pain in her heart and a merry laugh on her lips, she would leap on to the tables and snap her fingers indiscriminately.

Often it was her duty to drink off glass after glass of champagne ; but she never became inebriated.[1] Her purpose in life was too set—she meant to break away. In Nicholas Klick's " Life of Anna Podd " he states that she met the Tsar at a ball, whence she was hired professionally. This statement is entirely untrue ; and I am more than surprised that such a talented man as Klick should have made such a grievous error.

It has been absolutely impossible to unearth the true story of her meeting with the Tsar.

[1] Except on one occasion. For particulars, see Boris Brattlevitch's " Women of Russia."

ANNA PODD

It was after their meeting that the real progress of her career commenced. Her Royal master established her in the palace as serving-maid to the ailing Tsarina—a generous but somewhat tactless act on his part. Somehow or other, history whispers, Anna fell foul of the Tsarina—they simply hated one another. Occasionally the Tsarina would throw hot water over Anna for sheer spite. Poor Anna, her beauty was alike her joy and her terror. The Tsarina, Klick informs us, was somewhat plain, and knew it—hence her distaste for the dazzling Anna.

One day, the Tsarina died—no one knew why. Anna, guileless and innocent enough, was at once suspected by all of having poisoned her, except the Tsar, who, to avert further suspicion, promptly created her Duchess of Poddoff. This mark of royal esteem had the effect of quieting the people for a while at least. Life went on much as usual at the Royal Palace. Anna was kept in close seclusion for safety's sake. The Tsar loved her with a steady, burning devotion which caused him to have all his children by the Tsarina rechristened " Anna," irrespective of sex.

A WITHERED NOSEGAY

One day a messenger arrived in blue and yellow uniform [1] to bid the Tsar gird himself for war. When the luckless Anna heard the news, she was with her women (all ladies of title) : some say she swooned ; others aver that she merely sat down rather suddenly. Fate had indeed dealt her a smashing blow. Once her Imperial lover left her side she would at once be taken prisoner and flung God knows where. This she knew instinctively, intuitively. Klick describes for us her dramatic scene with the Tsar.

"He was just retiring to bed," he writes, "preparatory to making an early start the next morning, when the door burst open, and Anna, tear-stained and sobbing, threw herself into the room and, hurling herself to the bed, flung herself at his feet, which, owing to his immensity of stature, were protruding slightly over the end of the mattress. 'Take me with you !' she cried repeatedly. 'No, no, no !' replied the Tsar equally repeatedly. At length, worn out by her pleading, the poor woman fell asleep. It was dawn when the Tsar, stepping

[1] According to Mettlethorp's "Asiatic Soldiery," vol. VII.

over her recumbent form, bade her a silent good-bye and went out to face unknown horror. Half an hour later Anna was flung into a dungeon, preceding her long and tiring journey to Siberia."

Thus Klick describes for us the pulsating horror of perhaps one of the most pitiful nights in Russian history.

In those days the journey to Siberia was infinitely more wearisome than it is now. Poor Anna ! She was conveyed so far in a litter, and so far in a sleigh, and when the prancing dogs grew tired she had perforce to walk. Heaven indeed have pity on those unfortunate women from whom the eye of an Emperor has been removed.

For thirty long years Anna slaved in Siberia. She drew water from the well, swept the floor of the crazy dwelling wherein she lived, lit the fire, and polished the samovar when necessary. In her heart the bird of hope occasionally fluttered a draggled wing : would he send for her—would he ? If only the war were ended ! But no ! Rumours came of fierce fighting near Itchbanhar, where the troops of General Codski were quartered. It was,

of course, the winter following the fearful siege of
Mootch. According to Brattlevitch in volume II. of
" War and Why," the General had arranged three
battalions in a " frat " or large semi-circle, in the
comparative shelter of a " boz " or low-lying hill,
in order to cover the stealthy advance of several
minor divisions who were thus able to execute a
miraculous " yombott " or flank movement, so as
to gain the temporary vantage ground of an adjacent
" bluggard " or coppice. All this, of course, though
having nothing materially to do with the life of Anna
Podd, goes to show the reader what a serious crisis
Russia was going through at the time.

It was fifteen years after peace was declared that
the Tsar sent a messenger to Siberia commanding
Anna's immediate release and return, and also con-
ferring upon her the time-honoured title of Podski.
Anna was hysterical with joy, and filled herself a
flask of vodka against the journey home. Poor Anna
—she was destined never to see St. Petersburg
again.

It was while they were changing sleighs at a wayside inn that she was attacked by a " mipwip " or

white wolf,[1] which consumed quite a lot of the hapless woman before any one noticed.

Brattlevitch tells us that the Tsar was utterly dazed by this cruel bereavement. He had Anna's remains embalmed with great pomp and buried in a public park, where they were subsequently dug up by frenzied anarchists.[2] He also conferred upon her in death the deeds and title of Poddioskovitch, thus proving how a poor cabaret girl rose to be one of the greatest ladies in the land.

[1] See Tadski's " Natural Mammals of the Steppes."
[2] During the celebrated rising in 1682.

SOPHIE, UNCROWNED QUEEN OF HENRY VIII

SOPHIE
From an old print

SOPHIE, UNCROWNED QUEEN OF HENRY VIII

CONTEMPORARY history tells us little of Sophie, later chronicles tell us still less, while the present-day historians know nothing whatever about her. It is only owing to concentrated research and indomitable patience that we have succeeded in unearthing a few facts which will serve to distinguish her from that noble band of unknown heroines who have lived, paid the price, and died, unnoted and unsung!

She was born at Esher. The name of her parents it has been impossible to discover, and as to what part of Esher she first inhabited we are also hopelessly undecided.

As a child some say she was merry and playful, while others describe her as solemn and morose. The reproduction on page 102 is from an old print discovered by some ardent antiquaries hanging upside down in a disused wharf at Wapping.

A WITHERED NOSEGAY

It was obviously achieved when she was somewhere between the ages of twenty and forty. The unknown artist has caught the fleeting look of ineffable sadness, as though she entertained some inward premonition of her destiny and her spirit was rebelling dumbly against what was inevitable.

Esher in those days was but a tiny hamlet—a few houses clustered here, and a few more clustered there. London, then a graceful city set upon a hill, could be seen on a clear day from the northernmost point of Esher. On anything but a clear day it was, of course, impossible to see it at all. Esher is now, and always has been, remarkable for its foliage. In those days, when the spring touched the earth with its joyous wand, all the trees round and about the village blossomed forth into a mass of green. The river wound its way through verdant meadows and pastures. In winter-time—providing that the frost was very strong—it would become covered in ice, thus forming a charming contrast to early spring and late autumn, when the rain was wont to transform it into a swirling torrent, which often, so historians tell us, rose so high that it overflowed its banks and caused much alarm to the inhabitants of Esher proper. We do not use the expression " Esher proper " from any prudish reason, but merely because Little Esher, a mile down the road, might in the reader's mind become a factor to promote muddle if we did not take care to indicate clearly its close proximity.

Esher, owing to its remarkable superabundance of trees, was in summer-time famous for its delightful variety of birds : magpies, jackdaws, thrushes and wagtails, in addition to the usual sparrows and tom-tits, were seen frequently ; occasionally a lark or a starling would charm the villagers with its song.

The soil of Esher, contrary to the usual supposition, was not as fertile as one could have wished. Often, unless planted at exactly the right time, fruit and vegetables would refuse to grow at all. The main road through Esher proper, passing later through Little Esher, was much used by those desiring to reach Portsmouth or Swanage or any of the Hampshire resorts. Of course, travellers wishing to visit Cromer or Southend or even Felixstowe would naturally leave London by another route entirely.

Dick Turpin was frequently seen tearing through

Esher, with his face muffled, and a large hat and a long cloak, riding a horse, at night—there was no mistaking him.

According to Sophie's diary, written by her every day with unfailing regularity for thirty-five years, she always just missed seeing Dick Turpin. This was apparently a source of great grief to her; often she would pause by the roadside and weep gently at the thought of him. Poor Sophie! One was to ride along that very road who was destined to mean much more to her than bold Dick Turpin. But we anticipate.

It was perhaps early autumn that saw Esher at its best—how brown everything was, and yet, in some cases, how yellow! As a hunting centre it was very little used, though occasionally a stag or a wild boar would, like Dick Turpin, pass through it.

One evening, when the trees were soughing in the wind and the sun had sunk to rest, Sophie went out with her basket. It was too late to buy anything, but she felt the need of air; not that the basket was necessary in order to obtain this, but somehow she felt she couldn't bear to be without it, such a habit had it become. The darkness was rapidly drawing in. Sophie paused and spoke to a frog she saw in a puddle ; it didn't answer, so she passed on.

Suddenly she heard from the direction of London the sound of hoofs ! " Dick Turpin ! " her heart cried, and she at once commenced to climb an elm the better to see him pass ; but it was not Dick Turpin— it was a shorter man with a beard. On seeing the intrepid girl, he reined in his roan chestnut-spotted filly. " Hi ! " he cried. Sophie slowly climbed down. " Who are you ? " she asked, after she had dusted the bark from her fichu. " Henry the Eighth ! " cried the man with a ready laugh, and, leaping off his charger, took her in his arms. " Oh, sire ! " she said, and would have swooned but that his strength upheld her. History tells us little about that interview. Suffice to say that later on Sophie walked gravely back to Esher proper, alas ! without her basket, but carrying proudly in her hand a brooch cunningly wrought into the shape of a raspberry.

It is known as an authentic fact that Sophie never saw her Royal lover again. He rode away that night perhaps to Woking, perhaps to Virginia Water—who knows ?

Sophie lived on in Esher until the age of thirty-nine, when she was taken to London and flung into the Tower, where she remained a closely guarded prisoner for a year. Every one loved her and used to visit her in her cell. She was exceedingly industrious, and managed to get through quite a lot of tatting during her captivity.

The day of her execution dawned fair over St. Paul's Cathedral. Sophie in her little cell rose early and turned her fichu. " Why do you do that ? " asked the gaoler. " Because I am going to meet my end," Sophie gently replied. The man staggered dumbly away, fighting down the lump which would come in his hardened throat.

When the time came Sophie left her cell with a light step. She walked to Tower Hill amidst a body of Beefeaters. " The way is long," she said bravely. Every Beefeater bowed his head.

There was a dense crowd round the scaffold. Sophie heeded them not ; she ran girlishly up the steps to where the executioner was leaning on his axe. " Where do I put my head ? " she asked simply. The executioner pointed to the block. " There ! " said he. " Where did you think you put it ? " Sophie reproved him with a look and knelt down. Then she gazed sweetly at the gaoler, who for a year had stinted her in everything. " The past is buried," she said sweetly. " To you I bequeath my tatting ! " With these charitable words still hovering on her lips, she laid her head upon the fatal block ; from that trying position she threw the executioner a dumb look. " Do your duty, my friend," she said, and shut her eyes and her mouth.

Mastering his emotion with an effort, the heads- man raised his axe ; through a mist of tears it fell.

"LA BIBI"

" LA BIBI "

From the pastel by Coddle

" LA BIBI "

HORTENSE POISSONS—" La Bibi." What memories that name conjures up ! The incomparable—the lightsome—the effervescent—her life—a rose-coloured smear across the history of France—her smile—tier upon tier of sparkling teeth—her heart, that delicate organ for which kings fought in the streets like common Dukes—but enough ; let us trace her to her obscure parentage. You all know the Place de la Concorde—she was not born there. You have all visited the Champs Elysées—she was not born there. And there's probably no one who doesn't know of the Faubourg St. Honoré—but she was not born there. Sufficient to say that she was born. Her mother, poor, honest, *gauche*, an unpretentious seamstress ; she seamed and seamed until her death in 1682 or 1683 : Bibi, at the age of ten, flung on to the world homeless, motherless, with nothing but her amazing beauty between her and starvation or worse. Who can blame her for what

she did—who can question or condemn her motives ?
She was alone. Then Armand Brochet (who shall
be nameless) entered the panorama of her career.
What was she to do—refuse the roof he offered her ?
This waif (later on to be the glory of France), this
leaf blown hither and thither by the winds of Destiny
—what was she to do ? Enough that she did.

Paris, a city of seething vice and corruption—her
home, the place wherein she danced her first catoucha,
that catoucha which was so soon to be followed by her
famous Japanese schottische, and later still by her
celebrated Peruvian minuet. Voltaire wrote a lot, but
he didn't mention her; Jean Jacques Rousseau
scribbled for hours, but never so much as referred
to her; even Molière was so reticent on the subject of
her undoubted charms that no single word about
her can be found in any of his works.[1]

Her life with Armand Brochet (who shall still be
nameless) three years before she stepped on to the
boards—how well we all know it! Her famous epigram
at the breakfast table : " Armand, my friend, this egg

[1] For full reference, see Dulwich Library—'buses Nos. 48
and 75 and L.C.C. trams ; change at Camberwell Green.

is not only soft—but damn soft." How that remark convulsed Europe!

Her first appearance on the stage was in Paris, 1690, at the Opéra. Bovine writes of her : " This airy, fairy thing danced into our hearts ; her movements are those of a gossamer gadfly—she is the embodiment of spring, summer, autumn and winter." By this one can clearly see that in a trice she had Paris at her feet—and what feet ! Pierre Dugaz, the celebrated chiropodist, describes them for us. " They were ordinary flesh colour," he tells us, " with blue veins, and toe-nails which, had they not been cut in time, would have grown several yards long and thus interfered with her dancing."

What a sidelight on her character !—gay, Bohemian, care-free as a child, not even heeding her feet, her means of livelihood. Oh, Bibi—" Bibi Cœur d'Or," as she was called so frequently by her multitudinous adorers—would that in these mundane days you could revisit us with your girlish laugh and supple dancing form ! Look at the portrait of her, painted by Coddle at the height of her amazing beauty : note the sensitive nostrils, the delicate little

mouth, and those eyes—the gayest, merriest eyes
that ever charmed a king's heart ; and her hair—
that " mass of waving corn," as Bloodworthy
describes it in his celebrated book of International
Beauties. But we must follow her through her
wonderful life—destined, if not to alter the whole
history of France, why not ?

After her appearance in Paris she journeyed to
Vienna, where she met Herman Veigel : you all
know the story of that meeting, so I will not enlarge
upon it—enough that they met. It was, of course,
before he wrote his " Ode to an Unknown Flower "
and " My Gretchen has Large Flat Ears," poems
which were destined to live almost for ever. Bibi
left Vienna and journeyed to London—London, so
cold and grim after Paris the Gay and Vienna the
Wicked. In her letter to Madame Perrier she says,
" My dear—London's awful " ; and " Ludgate
Circus—I ask you ! " But still, despite her dislike
of the city itself, she stayed for eight years, her whole
being warmed by the love and adulation of the
populace. She appeared in the ballet after the opera.
" Her dancing," writes Follygob, " is unbelievable,

incredible ; she takes one completely by surprise—
her Butterfly dance was a revelation." This from
Follygob. Then Henry Pidd wrote of her, " She
is a woman." This from H. Pidd !

Then back to Paris—home, the place of her birth.
Fresh conquests. In November, 1701, she intro-
duced her world-famed Bavarian fandango, which
literally took Paris by storm—it was in her dressing-
room afterwards that she made her celebrated
remark to Maria Pipello (her only rival). Maria
came ostensibly to congratulate her on her success,
but in reality to insult her. " *Ma petite*," she said,
sneering, " *l'hibou, est-il sur le haie?* " Quick as
thought Bibi turned round and replied with a gay
toss of her curls, " *Non, mais j'ai la plume de ma
tante !* " Oh, witty, sharp-tongued Bibi ! A word
must be said of the glorious ballets she originated
which charmed France for nearly thirty years.
There were " Life of a Rain Drop," " Hope Triumphant," and " Angels Visiting Ruined Monastery
at Night." This last was an amazing creation for
one so uneducated and uncultured as La Jolie Bibi ;
people flocked to the Opéra again and again in order

to see it and applaud the ravishing originator. Then came her meeting with the King in his private box. We are told she curtsied low, and, glancing up at him coyly from between her bent knees, gave forth her world-renowned epigram, " *Comment va, Papa?* " Louis was charmed by this exquisite exhibition of drollery and *diablerie*, and three weeks later she was brought to dance at Versailles. This was triumph indeed—La Belle Bibi was certainly not one to miss opportunities. A month later she found herself installed at Court—the King's Right Hand. Then began that amazing reign of hers— short lived, but oh, how triumphant, dukes, duchesses, countesses, even princes, paying homage at the feet of La Bibi the dancer, now Hortense, Duchesse de Mal-Moulle! Did she abuse her power? Some say she did, some say she didn't; some say she might have, some say she might not have; but there is no denying that her beauty and gaiety won every heart that was brought into contact with her. Every after-noon regularly Louis was wont to visit her by the private staircase to her apartments; together they would pore over the ways and campaigns of war drawn up and submitted by the various generals. Then when Louis was weary Bibi would put the maps in the drawer, draw his head on to her breast, and sing to him songs of her youth, in the attractive cracked voice that was the bequest of her mother who used to sing daily whilst she seamed and seamed. Meanwhile, intrigue was placing its evil fingers upon the strings of her fate. Lampoons were launched against her, pasquinades were written of her; when she went out driving, fruit and vegetables were often hurled at her. Thus were the fickle hearts of the people she loved turned against their Bibi by the poisonous tongues of those jealous courtiers who so ardently sought her downfall.

You all know the pitiful story of her fall from favour—how the King, enraged by the stories he had heard of her, came to her room just as she was going to bed.

" You've got to go," he said.

" Why ? " she answered.

History writes that this ingenuous remark so unmanned him that his eyes filled with tears, and he dashed from the room, closing the door after him in order that her appealing eyes might not cause him to deflect from his purpose.

Poor Bibi—your rose path has come to an end, your day is nearly done. Back to Paris, back to the squalor and dirt of your early life. Bibi, now in her forty-seventh year, with the memories of her recent splendours still in her heart, decided to return to the stage, to the public who had loved and fêted her. Alas! she had returned too late. Something was missing—the audience laughed every time she came on, and applauded her only when she went off. Oh, Bibi, Bibi Cœur d'Or, even now in this cold age our hearts ache for you. Volauvent writes in the *Journal* of the period : " Bibi can dance no longer." Veaux caps it by saying " She never could," while S. Kayrille, well known for his wit and kindly humour, reviewed her in the Berlin *Gazette* of the period by remarking, in his customarily brilliant manner, " She is very plain and no longer in her first youth." This subtle criticism of her dancing, though convulsing the Teutonic capital, was in reality the cause of her leaving the stage and retiring with her one maid to a small house in Montmartre, where history has it she petered out the last years of her eventful career.

Absinthe was her one consolation, together with a miniature of Louis in full regalia. Who is this haggard wretch with still the vestiges of her wondrous beauty discernible in her perfectly moulded features ? —not La Belle Bibi ! Oh, Fate—Destiny—how cruel are you who guided her straying feet through the mazes of life ! Why could she not have died at her zenith—when her portrait was painted ?

But still her gay humour was with her to the end. As she lay on her crazy bed, surrounded by priests, she made the supreme and crowning *bon mot* of her brilliant life. Stretching out her wasted arm to the nearly empty absinthe bottle by her bed, she made a slightful resentful *moue* and murmured " *Encore une !* "

Oh, brave, witty Bibi !

GLOSSARY

BALOONA, ENRIQUE. Artist and *dilettante*, famous for his "Portrait of Isabella Angelica," "Spanish Peaks," and "Half-caste Child with Orange."

BEN-HEPPLE, NICHOLAS. Eighteenth century historian. Author of "Julie de Poopinac" (17 vols.).

BLOODWORTHY, STEPHEN. Author of "International Beauties," "Then and Now," and "Now and Then."

BOTTIBURGEN, HANS VON. Science master, Munich College. Author of "Our Women," "Do Actresses Mind Much?" and "Life of Fritz Schnotter" (3 vols.).

BOTTLE, ELIZABETH. Adapter and translator of several works of the period.

BOVINE, GUSTAVE. Author of "French without Tears" and "Vive les Vacances," etc.

BRAMP, NORMAN. Author of "Up and Away," "Reynard, the Story of a Fox," "Tantivoy," and "Female Influence and Why?" (5 vols.).

BRAMPENRICH, FRITZ. German historian.

BRATTLEVITCH, BORIS. Russian author. Books: "War and Why," "Women of Russia." Several good cooking recipes.

BUG, REGINALD. Actor—occasional property man. Parts he played: "Romeo," "Bottom," "Third Guest" in "The Berlin Girl," "Norman" in "Oh, Charles—a Satire on the

A WITHERED NOSEGAY

Massacre of Saint Bartholomew," and others. Hobbies: Cup-and-ball, tilting, and fretwork.

CABALLERO, BASTA. Actor and founder of "Shakespearean Theatre" in Barcelona.

CAMPANELE, VITTORIO. Florentine engraver. "Early Portrait of Bianca di Pianno-Forti," "Raised Pansies on China Plaque," etc.

CARLINI, ANGELO. Italian actor—formerly plumber during the Renaissance.

CHUGGSKI, DIMITRI. Russian actor.

CODDLE, HUMPHREY. Artist, well known for his "Cows Grazing outside Dover," "Playmates," and "Daddy's Darling."

CRONK, OSWALD, BART. Painter of "Madcap Moll, Eighth Duchess of Wapping," "Pine Trees near Ascot," and "Esther Lollop as 'Cymbeline.'"

DENTIFRICE, PIERRE. Actor—French (early).

DUGAZ, PIERRE. Court chiropodist, seventeenth century. Author of "Feet and Fashion," "The Valley of Waving Corns," etc.

FIBINIO, PIETRO. Italian—author of "Bianca," "God Bless the Pope," etc.

FOLLYGOB, ALAN. English Dramatic Critic. Clubs: "The Union Jack" and "The What-Ho" in Jermyn Street.

GERPHIPPS, RONALD. Very old Scotch painter—famous for "Portrait of Maggie McWhistle," "Evening on Loch Lomond," and "Glasgow, my Glasgow!"

GOETHE. Obscure German author. Suspected of having written "Faust."

GLOSSARY

GROBMAYER, CARL. Early German etcher.

GRUNDELHEIM. PAUL. German author and historian. Principal works : " Toilers who have Toiled," " Women of Wurtemburg," and " Byways of the Black Forest."

KAYRILLE, SIEGFRIED. Born Berlin, 1670. Disappointed playwright, and subsequent art critic.

KLICK, NICHOLAS. Russian—author of " Life of Anna Podd " (6 vols.), and " Was Ivan Terrible ? "

MACTWEED, SANDY. Scotch actor of some note.

MARY, BLOODY. Queen of England.

METTLETHORP, RUPERT. Compiler of " Asiatic Soldiery " (23 vols.).

PIDD, HENRY. Severe dramatic critic—English.

POLATA, JOSÉ. Professor—Spanish. Author of " From Girl to Woman," " Spanish Olives, and How," etc., etc.

POLIOLIOLI, GUISEPPE. Author of " Women of Italy " and " Nelly of Naples," a musical comedy of the period.

PUNTER, AUGUSTUS. Seventeenth century painter, famous for " Sarah, Lady Tunnell-Penge, with Dog," " Gravesend by Night," and various crayon portraits, notably " A Merry Girl " and " The Drowsy Sentry."

ROUSSEAU, JEAN JACQUES. French writer of some note. See Carlyle's " French Revolution."

SCHNOTTER, FRITZ. German actor, sixteenth century.

SHEEPMEADOW, EDGAR. English writer—author of " Beds and their Inmates " (18 vols.), " The Corn Chandler," " Women Large and Women Small " (10 vols.).

TADSKI, SERGE. Early, fairly. Russian. Author and compiler of the following : " Russian Realism," " Natural

Mammals of the Steppes," " Flora and Fauna of Siberia," etc., and light verse.

TOSSELE, YVONNE, MME. First female mezzotinter of the Revolutionary Era.

TURPIN, DICK. Highwayman—English. Inventor of straw sunhats for hot horses.

VEAUX, PAUL. Art critic—Paris.

VEIGEL, HERMAN. German poet—famous for " Twilight Fancies," " There *was* a Garden," and " Collected Poems, including ' The Ballad of Crazy Bertha.' "

VOLAUVENT, ARMAND. Art critic—Paris.

VOLTAIRE (Christian name unknown). Old writer—French.

WAFFLE, RAYMOND. Georgian writer. Author of " Our Dogs," " Canine Cameos," and " Pretty Rover, the Story of a Boarhound."

PRESS NOTICES

" *Clagmouth Chronicle* " :—" A book to be taken up and put down again."

" *East Bromley Advertiser* " :—" This is a book ! "

" *The Girls' Globe* " :—" Every young girl should read this."

Doctor Cheval in " *Advice to a Mother* " :—" No bedside table is complete without ' A Withered Nosegay.' "

Joe Bogworth in " *Capital and Labour* " says :—" This book is perhaps the greatest power for good or evil in democratic England. Though obviously the work of a thinker, should it by any chance fall into the wrong hands it would go far towards undermining not only the League of Nations, but the London County Council to boot ! "

Aunt Hilda in " *Fireside Fun* " says :—" Darling Chicks, get your mumsie to buy you ' A Withered Nosegay ' for your birthday."

Lady Minerva Stuffe in " *Undies* " writes :—" Well-dressed women will eagerly peruse these fascinating memoirs."

" *The Playing Field* " :—" ' Chaps ! ' Read this book."

" *The Political Gazette* " :—" Well done, Noel Coward ! Bravo, Lorn Macnaughtan ! "

Herr von Grob in " *The Austrian Tyrol* " :—" Gott in Himmel ! "

" *Chicken Chat* " :—" I advise keen poultry keepers to buy and read ' A Withered Nosegay.' "

A WITHERED NOSEGAY

" *Cri de Paris* " :—" Ce livre n'est pas seulement stupide, mais c'est excessivement irritant, et absolument sans humeur." (Translation : " This book is not only charming, but it is excessively entertaining and brilliantly humorous.")

" *Claybank Courier* " :—" Once read—never forgotten."

" *Wigan World* " :—" Splendid for those just learning to read."

" *Boxing Weekly* " :—" Dam' good ! "

CHELSEA BUNS

BY
HERNIA WHITTLEBOT

EDITED BY
NOEL COWARD

WITH AN INTRODUCTION BY
GASPARD PUSTONTIN

PORTRAIT OF MISS WHITTLEBOT, EXECUTED IN THE
SPRING OF 1924 BY G. E. CALTHROP.

Portrait in the possession of Miss Barnett.

NOTE

My thanks are due to the Editors of
The Bristol Trumpet, *Freedom*, and *Sex
Weekly* for their kind permission in
allowing me to reprint certain of the
poems in this volume.

HERNIA WHITTLEBOT.
SOUTHSEA, 1924.

CONTENTS

Contents

FOREWORD

There can be no two opinions about Miss Whittlebot's work. She has steadily climbed the precarious ladder of Poetic Conquest, and from the height of her unassailable pinnacle she now bestows upon an eagerly expectant public this new proof of her iridescent genius.

There is something flamboyant in her gallantly coloured phraseology—she affects one like " Jumbles " or a merry-go-round in a Turkish bath.

She scatters the tepid tea-leaves of Victorian Aspiration and Georgian achievement with the incisive *mesquinerie* of a literary Bonaparte.

Nothing is spared the flail of her titulative satire. The carcaphanous charm of Harlequin and Columbine evaporates like withered potpourri before the on-coming hurricane of her merciless pen. Hostesses retire battered, to the sombre tranquillity of the de Goncourts, and the *baroque* naughtiness of Madame de Sévigné.

In the puerile deprecations of her poetic contemporaries one senses the lurking and resentful machinations of wheels within wheels. They rise to the elusive bait of her audacity as crayfish to a noc-turnal lantern—only to discover that in the searching illumination of her mental causticism their very vices are twisted into mediocre virtues ; and they sink back abashed to find solace and consolation in the healing balm of their own particular satellites.

In France, Hernia Whittlebot has been hailed and extolled even more perhaps than in England. Within the obscure translucent gloom of the Bois members of the Whittlebot " cult " may be observed wandering like contented spirits temporarily released from the narrow confines of ungarlanded graves, and in their shining eyes the knowledge that at last they have found the source of life's inspiration.

To those larger sections of the British reading public to whom Marcel Proust is but a conversational hair-net, the name of Gaspard Pustontin will naturally wake no responsive enthusiasm. Therefore I feel it necessary in a brief résumé to expose the salient features of his picturesque career.

Though his work is distractingly modern, he is by no means a young man. Born at St. Jean-sur-Fiscque in 1870, educated at Mintes-le-Pon, and imprisoned at Chaize (for peculiar behaviour in the Simplon tunnel), his private life is not surprisingly thrown upon the drab screen of public opinion in furious bas-relief.

He commenced writing at an early age. All *littérateurs* are cognisant with the fin de siècle finesse of his *Mon Père n'a pas de Bottes*, and later his *Toutes les Neurotiques sont en haut* (Bandeau Frères, Paris, France).

His short adulatory preface to CHELSEA BUNS will assuredly give Miss Whittlebot's work an additional *cachet* in Parisian circles, but in England, where his *Poésie* is as yet a *chanson inconnue*, I am proud to be the first to write his name.

NOEL COWARD.

1924.

To *Mademoiselle Hernia Whittlebot*

J'éprouve beaucoup de plaisir à poser
aux pieds de Mademoiselle Whittlebot
cette épreuve de mon admiration la plus
sincère.

Je me souviens de mon enfance, ma
première vue d'un papillon, rouge, noir,
et vert aussi me souviens-je d'une chatte
affolée.

Entre ces mémoires éblouissantes votre
tête acharnée se heurte contre les murs de
ma sensibilité. Il est extraordinaire que
lorsque deux Génies se rencontrent dans
l'espace, les liens invisibles s'enlacent,
et la flamme qui provient de l'étreinte
s'envole jusqu'aux près de l'Olympe.

La piquante sorcellerie de votre esprit
se détache nettement des chinoiseries de
l'hurluberlu moderne. Prestidigitateurs

en mots dégoûtants, la portée desquels ils ignorent—aspirants ignobles à une gloire lugubre, ils se tordent dans le miasme puant de leur propre grandiloquence.

Je remercie les Muses Poétiques de la fraîcheur de votre simplicité. Comme la Lune sur les eaux, votre voix rhythmique se mêle à mes reflections mélancoliques, et je pâme aux sons gracieux de vos Quatrains diaboliques.

GASPARD PUSTONTIN.

CHELSEA BUNS

NEUROTIC THOUGHTS ON THE RENAISSANCE

He's in the Lancers, sir, she said,
Sir, she said, sir, she said.
He prances high on horses yellow :
Trundle, trundle, hearty fellow.

Sugar mice like billiard balls
Go skit-a-wit,
Mouthed to nothingness
With infantile paralysis.

Silly, painted shrieks
Snick through the constipated air.

Her baize-green face
Glares treacle sweet
Down wounded hills,
With chuckling gorse a-murmur,
With the indiscreet avowals
Of sadic curates in their laity.

TO A MAIDENHAIR FERN

You pretty thing,
Each dainty frond unbending,
Supple unending,
    Like pearls on a string—
Your message is sending
    A promise of spring.

NOUS N'AVONS PLUS DE CHICHI

Chelsea streets are trim and grand,
Trams are fortresses of pride,
And the tortoiseshell cat of the violinist
Stalks mincingly through the ordure.
I string my beads of parrot sound,
And clap my soignées mental hands,
A-loop the loop—they swing and float,
Immeasurably sensible—
Gauds in the aquarium of some vast in-
    finitude,
Globe-like breasts of tender Americans
Glimmer through the fragile night
" A party in this lovely house.
How darling heavenly ! "
The Town Hall's still there,
Godstone green and Purtle red,
And all the poets spew their potted
    shrimps
And don the velvet boots of turpitude.

Along the thundering pavement roars
    and screams
A mouse—inclining to " The Good
    Intent "
For conversation's toasted cheese—
Salisbury plain and twopence coloured.
A country joke, ha-ha—ho-ho—ha-ha !
The Restoration plays were *far* the best.
Let us be humorous and so obscure,
Because our minds of rainbow-coloured
    clay
Insist on Marcel-wavèd friends
And blameless notoriety ;
Our hair drips this and that way with
    the wind
Of shrill falsetto sycophantic laughs.
Ha ! let's be bawdy with our Oxford
    wits,
And pornographic in a foreign tongue,
And flick away the genius of an age
With Nuttall's Etymology.
Pass the spotted dog,
Which looks like Aunt Maria's belly !

CONTOURS

Round—oblong—like jam—
Terse as virulent hermaphrodites ;
Calling across the sodden twisted ends
    of Time.
Edifices of importunity
Sway like Parmesan before the half-tones
Of Episcopalian Michaelmas ;
Bodies are so impossible to see in retro-
    spect—
And yet I know the well of truth
Is gutted like pratchful Unicorn.
Sog, sog, sog—why is my mind amphi-
    bious ?
That's what it is.

GUAVA JELLY

Anne Boleyn, you were not half so bold
As those who whispered of your sensi-
    bility,
And trickling through the corner of a
    biscuit tin,
The india-rubber leaves fly click-a-clack;
For Henry was a man of passing tender-
    ness,
With spheroid hands that groped away
    your dreams
Fantastical, elliptical his slavering lips,
Like cherry tart.
Puritanical were the forest trees;
And, ah! the sharpness of the moon's
    decay,
With oblong beams adrift in sensuality,
Came drifting through the purlieus of
    your soul.

GARIBALDI

Immaculately fine
　Like Elderberry wine,
　　And old Tokay's decline ;

Impassioned as a bog,
　Cavorting like a dog
　　Or brindled gollywog ;

Resembling the short
　Thin lessons we were taught
　　Of lazy battles fought ;

Grandiloquent we see,
　In all simplicity,
　　The trousered bumble-bee.

And all the afternoon
　Disgruntled colonels swoon
　　Like wafers of the moon ;

And tea-cups, dancing, pass
  Along the azure grass
    To where the monkey was.

The stilted elfin talk
  Like buttered tomahawk
    Destroys the Deacon's stalk.

Unfathomable, deep,
  The pornographic sheep
  Like bus conductors creep.

Interminable, boring,
  Like festooned launches snoring
    From Maidenhead to Goring.

FAMILY CIRCLE

A table spread
With vegetarian naughtiness,
Lasciviously the Burgundy
Grunts to see.
The Petite Suisse
Is no less pale
Than botched poetic faces
Thick as cream
That's curdled in the telling.
The saucy butler hovers
With blue-veined legs
A-twitch with varicose ambiguity ;
Spatulate hands nark
At the multicoloured gems
Of still-born conversation.
" We'll give a grand recital Tuesday
        week "
With marmaladed fingers plaiting dreams
Of conquering blasts among beslaugh-
        tered literature.

Blind drunk with stale achievement,
Seeking more to rend with elephantine
    fingers
Some poor web of silly weed
Athwart a stagnant pool
Of excellently bred ability ;
Scorbutic brains, a-grapple and a-swoon,
Mazed with good living and effusive
    friends,
They keek and preen among the scented
    woofs
Bewoven for their ultimate decline
Towards the sullen breast of mediocrity.

SILLY BOY

Wait, I must wash my hands in rasp-
    berry beer.
  The saucepan's azure face sheds Anda-
    lusian beams
According to the segregating tears
  Of wayside urchins on St. Crispin's
    day.
Devotedly I hope that you are well—
  Your asthma better? Good.
And now your teeth—
  Paradoxical is the pain of life,
Spatulate, transcendent,
  Empujamos la mesa.

CANDELABRA

Things come into your mind
And are gone again
Like drops of silly, truculent rain.
Do I like butter?
Who am I to question Nature's sanctity?
Ah! gorgeous, gorgeous is the sun,
Shining out loud with a rum-tum-tum;
I stretch my naked limbs and writhe
About the desiccated drive—
Which doesn't rhyme with writhe, but
    still,
Without the " a " saliva will.

CHILDREN'S TALES

(1)

My mother said to me :
Beware of gipsies bold,
Who lure you with their cold
Tight fingers to where the wood
Is spatulate and thin,
Like eager casks of tawny port im-
 placable.

(2)

My mother said to me :
The brindled cow has taken up
A Kreisler theme in G ;
The posturing moon
Is thrilling like a maiden for her lover's
 touch ;
And, ah ! see how

The brindled cow
Importunate
Prepares evasive legs to mark the rhyme.
A little dog, hysteria unchained,
With raucous grunts goes lolling o'er the
    downs.
The willow-pattern dish to Gretna Green
Must fly
And sigh
A threnody.
Leave out the spoon, it doesn't mean a
    thing.

(3)

My mother said to me :
Clinkerty clank clonk,
Clinkerty clank clonk,
Clonderloo.
Felinity, enstrangled in the treacly depths
Of turgidity,
Who with forceful red hands
Has sealed with sharp masculinity
Her mousing conquests ?
Little Tommy Thin.

(4)

My mother said to me—
A flaxen figure, glassy hair a-spin,
And broken as a doll;
The yielding green of darkling
    spears
Abandoned to her sad posterior
A bowl like cod's eyes,
Sharp and thin;
Chalcedony and agate waferous May
    blossom
Floating in and out,
Like country vicars' wives
Intent on deadly kindnesses.
Obstetrically scientific
Like the motherhood of spinsters
Behind the cashmere veils,
Phantasmagoric, gluttonous.
With fervent tentacles agrasp,
Beside the custard hot and green,
On, on the wooden article aglaze,
The sunset's haze
Amaze;

The foxgloves nodding on in-
   adequate stalk :
I think I shall get out and walk.

(5)

My mother said to me—
The angular extremities
Of glaring thin tin mugs,
Apocryphal, dynamic,
In matricate dythiambics
Rock, choke, creak :
Wednesday week
Will be the birthday of the Infanta.

(6)

My mother said to me—
In harlequined fancy
Pantaloon,
With conventional red-hot poker
Prodding the hopes of Messalinian
   adolescence :
Rock-a-bye baby.

WRITTEN FROM A MANSARD WINDOW IN A VELVET DRESS

Tell me your mouth is yellow,
  I will laugh—
Flinging high the loofah in the bath,
  Exacting measured honey from the
    sluice.
Ah well-a-day !

VICTORIAN RHAPSODY FOR LESSER MINDS

They're so attractive, flowers under glass ;
   The little waxen buds are *too* divine !
Those dear, delicious snowstorms are
   such fun—
   Amusing, don't you think ?
I've got a beaded footstool—such a dear.
Intriguing bubbles on a chandelier
Give me *such* inspiration for my work—
   So subtle, darling,
I've only eaten syllabubs for years.
Daguerreotypes *are* jolly—one appears
   Ineffably bucolic.
   Oh, to be different !
Give me an antimacassar for my dress
And several chignons for my happiness.

SPOTTED LILIES

Hey, hey, let her go,
With clicking heels and furbelow,

With welcome written on the mat
And little pebbles round and fat,

And all the dust of Purgatory,
And flatulent streams,

From the mustard depths
Of old men's beards.

Shallow fishes fly about my eyes,
Exacting toll like dragon-flies.

Of all the thoughts the best insure
The almond-coloured paramour.

Call back the cattle, Mary, dear,
Like aged festering potentates,

Their horns as posters on a hoarding,
Flaunting their tattered nonchalance;

The hermits in their caves of glass
(My breasts are round and square and
    green).

Clorinda's cracked the soup tureen.
Bring cigarettes and matches fat.

As ballet dancers' legs,
Golf-croquet is like daisies' eyes—

Whirling, twirling ecstasies,
Invertebrate—mausades—bodeuses—
    moqueuses.

Where are my garters?

MRS. GIBBON'S DECLINE AND
FALL

Sibilant apples glistering now
In your mauve hands,
Like priests that hold a tortoise to their
    mouth,
And Macabre days of tan and blue
Go hopping one, two, three.
Good God, it's time for tea !

SUNDAY MORNING AT WIES-BADEN

I sometimes think that shrimps and
    sprats
Should wear enormous Homburg hats,
And swim about with cricket bats
    Suspended from their ears.

Importunate the rolling downs,
Like very rude provincial clowns,
In knitted Jaeger dressing-gowns
    Upon the ends of piers.

MISERICORDIA

My breasts have sprung to meet you like
    the moon,
The nodding kingcups set my head
    aswoon.
If it were not Whit-Monday afternoon
I'd take a corrugated tinsel spoon,
Coagulate as golden macaroon,
Beat syncopated passion as a coon
Would write the honeyed phrase of Lorna
    Doone . . .
What matters it if Love be over soon ?

TO MY LITERARY PARASITES

I'll give you wooden phrases—
Words for horses—
Mechanical contrivances.
You give me adulation—emulation—
And dribble at my feet.
What's it to you ?
You've had the Russian Ballet !

TO BADRULBADOR FRAMPTON

The Day of Judgment crackling down
The hills of time,
Like mother going to her bath—
One for sorrow, two for joy ;
Like any little carking boy
Whose sex unfolding, calls to mind
The water-melon purity
Of Mrs. Hodgson's chignon,
Netted like a grape ;
And gardeners' corduroys
All mottled by the verisimilitude
Of passing horses.
I think a swan has leather kidneys !

CONTEMPORARY THOUGHT

Stravinsky, let me clutch your hand,
    And nuzzle at your breast,
The golden road to Samarkand
    Has made me so depressed.
Picasso, with your painted soul,
    Inspire me with a glance—
A flaunting Gauguin carmagnole
    Has set my pen a-dance.
Hey-ho, hey-ho, hey-hominy-ho,
    With a which and a what
And a where shall we go ?

SEND ME MY HAT

Sob your heart out, child of mine,
   And fling away your train ;
The clock is striking half-past nine
   And I must go to Spain ;
The speckled flowers incarnadine
   Will ease the body's pain.
      Grub
      Grub
      Grub
The tuck-shop bell is ringing
      And
      Swinging,
Ding-a-ding-a-dinging.

Athwart the fat bald head
Of Mr. Ebenezer Satterthwaite,

With small lascivious tartlets
     On
     A
     Plate.

For all the world like withered Mr. Keats
Tossing on high the multi-coloured
     sweets
Of villanelle's intoxicated muse.
I will not hear a word against the Jews,
     As,
     After
     All,
     They've
     Done
     A lot
     Of
     Good.
What's the use of grumbling—we should
On all occasions, like some striped
     rocking-horse,
All pull our weight around the garish
     course
Of life's betattered race.

The King and Queen not there—how
    strange !
       To range
Without a bowler hat on Derby Day.

THEME FOR OBOE IN E FLAT

Zebubbah zebubbah,
Zooboom tweet tweet,
Pidwiddy pidwiddy,
Pidantipatiddy.

Dark—round—
Suggestive beads of sound.

Zebubbah zebubbah,
Tweet tweet.

OLEOGRAPH

A cottage in the westering sun
   (This is my real mind speaking now),
The curling smoke when day is done,
The happy-hearted children run
To help their father pull the plough.
   If only peace were not so sad,
And happiness of rose-white youth
Were stained to glory mouth to mouth,
   I'd feel my heart serenely glad,
Would only intellect allow
(This is my real mind speaking now).

An
anthology
by

NOËL COWARD

★

SPANGLED

UNICORN

★

A selection from the
works of

ALBRECHT DRAUSLER

SERGE LLIAVANOV

JANET URDLER

ELIHU DUNN

ADA JOHNSTON

JANE SOUTHERBY DANKS

TAO LANG PEE

E. A. I. MAUNDERS

CRISPIN PITHER

JUANA MANDRAGÁGITA
(Translated by Lawton Drift)

NOËL COWARD

CONTENTS

CONTENTS

PREFACE

In selecting and arranging (and in some cases) translating this anthology I have been actuated solely by one dominant idea. That idea being, in a word "Progress". Progress on and up as opposed to Along and Down. Progress towards a goal still beyond our actual vision but nevertheless luminous and radiant in those rare moments of inspiration which come to the aid of every real Artist be he either Poet, Painter or Musician. There is a War to be won and a Gulf to be bridged. The War lies between the creative Artists and the Philistines, the Gulf lies between To-day and To-morrow.

In this slim volume I have gathered together from all parts of the world fragments of thought, rich in beauty, the fruits of minds that are unafraid, clear and incisive in sophistication, strong in awareness of the age in which they live. Uncompromising in the integrity of their standards. Civilisation, for all those who have eyes to see, is passing through a period of Flux and Counter Flux. Values to-day as concrete as the Pyramids, to-morrow will prove to be ephemeral as smoke. Nations rock and tremble and rock again, fissures appear in the granite of accepted conventions and far away, down the wind, can be heard the voice of the people. Change and interchange and counterchange, something stirring far far below tradition consciousness, more positive and absolute than revolution as we know it—immeasurable in its portent insistent, challenging as the waves of the sea—relentless.

LIST OF ILLUSTRATIONS

Janet Urdler

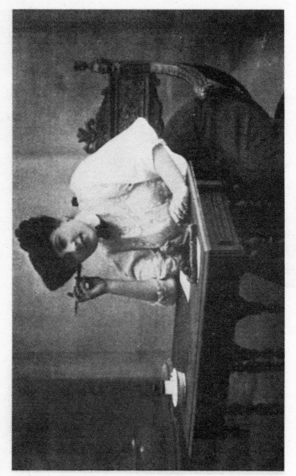

JANET URDLER

JANET URDLER

≈

INTRODUCTORY NOTE

JANET URDLER was born in Exeter on a
very bleak day in November 1887. Her
childhood was grim and church-ridden,
nothing stirred in her consciousness of
things other, until 1900 when she was taken
to Dawlish in a bullock cart. It was apparently a sort of picnic. Later she was forced
unwillingly to teach in school, and it was
during these years of bondage that her
"awareness" developed. Child psychology
interested her, but obscurely, she seldom
inflicted punishments on her pupils and she
was remotely popular but in no way
idolised.

When her mother and father died she
left Exeter and wandered. There are few
records of her journeyings; she was in

Lisbon in 1908 and Carthage the following
October. In 1912 she met Laura Todd (the
" Ariadne " of her early sonnets) and they
apparently went to Norway for a while.
When they returned War was sweeping
Europe. In an extract from a letter to Laura
in 1916 Janet says : " It is lovely here, very
peaceful and grey with rooks cawing, and
I suppose I am happy."

It was not until September 1920 that her
first book of Poems was published. Since
then she has written intermittently. *Lovers
of Brass*, in 1924, solidified her reputation,
which was further enhanced by *Bindweed* in
1927.

In an analysis of her work it is difficult
to avoid the obvious comparison with
Theodore Lange. There is the same twisted
earth consciousness and an almost identical
viewpoint on peasant maternity, but here I
venture to suggest the similarity ceases.
Whereas Lange (in everything but ' *The
Diver* ') was definitely retrogressive, Janet
Urdler goes forward and upward. The
three selected pieces in this book typify her

emancipation from the formal, in '*Hungry Land*', '*Hen bane, No Hen*' has been criticised as being reactionary, but to my mind, and I honestly believe this view is shared by most of her important contemporaries, this sudden spurt of almost sentimental irony is essential in illustrating the inverse ratio of the context. I have included '*Reversion to the Formal*' for no particular reason except that as an exhibition of verbal pyrotechnics it is immensely valuable, demonstrating as it does the importance of complete freedom of line. '*How does your Garden Grow?*' is too well known to require comment from me, or indeed anybody else.

JANET URDLER

REVERSION TO THE FORMAL

EMMA housemaid sees the shepherdess shepherdess with crook lambs' tails up crying up
trying gate hinges creak scream soul hinges
scream creak no love no love Emma housemaid round red hands chimney smokes at
sunset blue beads in thick sentimental air
with children near women's children spheri-
cal butter skins and legs sausage swollen
Job the Ploughman big Job big Job more
children nuzzling and crying mother Emma
mother Emma Emma no mother no love
no love dairy-fed produce lush pasturage
gate hinges scream creak happy scream
love scream women scream Job goes home
laughing Job big laughing Job windows
shut door shut hot body hot air Emma
housemaid no love waiting no love lonely.

JANET URDLER

HOW DOES YOUR GARDEN GROW

SILLY lady with your trowel
Consecrating female energy
On small male plants
Outside your garden wall
Plains stretch limbless
To odd horizons
Inside there is peace
Sequestered foolish tranquillity
Shut away from vital urge
Stupid Arabis
Sanctimonious Hollyhocks
Bestial Lobelias
Concealing their obscenity in Prettiness
Like Vicar's daughters
In Organdie
What is there above but sky
What is there beneath but earth

Thick hot earth alive with jostling seedlings
And strange lewd bulbs
Silly lady with your trowel
How does your garden grow?

JANET URDLER

HUNGRY LAND

EARTH in chains and hunger
Tadpoles in Ponds
Cows retching
Drought
Famine
Milko
Oh No
Cattle come home
No home
Speed the Plough
No Plough
Hen bane
No Hen
Night shade
No shade
Only Night
Hungry Night

Elihu Dunn

ELIHU DUNN

ELIHU DUNN

❧

INTRODUCTORY NOTE

ELIHU DUNN was born in Washington D.C. in 1896. He was educated there and then went West, then came back South. He was graduated from Deklopfer Burns High in 1920 New Orleans University A.B. 1924 Hoboken A.M. 1926, while in high school he attracted a good deal of attention, missed winning the inter-collegiate Poetry Contest prize by a hair's breadth 1923—1924—1925—1926—1927. Published *Blue Grass* 1928, *Blue Grass Revisited* 1929, *Blue Grass Again* 1930.

James Maddern Waller wrote of Elihu Dunn in 1929 " This man is a giant, the music of his words Crystallises in the air like bird song, he is the mouthpiece of his race calling them on to victory." Surely no greater tribute could be paid to any constructive poet. The selections from his work contained in this volume I think can truthfully be said to represent more or less comprehensively Dunn's strangely powerful race obsession. He is the champion of a cause and will always be just that. To expect him to write without bias would be as absurd as to demand Meredith Flood to compose chamber music. There is no compromise in these men.

ELIHU DUNN

NECROMANCY

MA skin is black
As an ole black crow
Ole black crow
Vo dodeo do
Ma Pap was white
As de wind blown snow
Wind blown snow
Vo dodeo do
Ma Mammy was brown
As chicken soup
Chicken soup
Boop oop a doop
She knocked my Pappy
For a loop
For a loop
Boop oop a doop
Ma sis is pale

As a piece of Gruyère
Piece of Gruyère
Halleluia
But ma skin's black
As an ole black crow
Ole black crow
Vo dodeo do.

ELIHU DUNN
      TO ROBERT ANDREWS

HARLEM

Yellow brown black
Limbs writhing in rhythm
Rhythm writhing limbs
Hot Momma Hey Hey
Where is Death if this is life
Night Life Night Death
Crazy 'bout you honey
Hey honey ma baby
African drums beatin' out soul rhythm
African blood coursing thru'
Dark streets
Hot dark breath
Shutters with light seepin' thru
Makin' black shadows
Black shadows of black loves
Saxophones moanin'

Groanin' groanin'
Where are de cotton fields
Where is dat blue grass
Where are dem ole oat cakes
No here Nigger
Hot Momma Hey Hey

ELIHU DUNN

MA PEOPLE

MA People
Call back ober yo shoulder
Way back to Jungle land
Come to Glory
Come with yo po hearts a-weary
Yo po souls a-stretchin' upwards to de light
Neber yo mind ma people
Neber yo mind when de white folks
Stand in the dusty streets a-nid noddin'
Der fool white heads
And a-laughin' and a-jeering'
De Lord lubs yo same as he lubs the King-
    fisher,
In de corn brakes
An de bees an de flowers in de Dixie fields
Ma people
Come on ma people

Lift up yo po hearts
Lift up yo po hands
Raise yo po eyes
The lord knows yo po backs is a-bendin'
Under yo po burden
An dat yo po feet is a-aching
In yo po shoes
Come on, yo po people
Ma People.

E. A. I. Maunders

E. A. I. MAUNDERS

E. A. I. MAUNDERS

୬ଡ଼

INTRODUCTORY NOTE

PREFACE TO LIFE

I AM me in one sense but not me in another sense because although sense is partially me it is not partially sense, but wholly sense, whereas I am not wholly me but partially me the sense of which is not sense entirely but too near truth to be not sense by which I mean that although not sense is far away from truth, truth is frequently not sense which makes me me more were it not that I was partially sense. Gertrude is Gertrude and I am me but we are the same in meaning, meaning being meaning to us and us being meaning to meaning and meaning meaning practically nothing to meaning people who are not people meaning Gertrude's bigness

is not my bigness any more than my littleness is Gertrude's littleness. Gertrude's
littleness is little littleness as her bigness is
big bigness because it is impossible for
Gertrude to do anything by halves because
her one-ness is too complete to be able to
conceive of Twoness and she is big big in
her bigness and not really little little in her
littleness whereas I can change as smallness
changes not because I am really small but
because I know smallness whereas Gertrude
does not know smallness but only bigness
in living bigly as diametrically opposed to
living smally which may or may not mean
not living at all inside but only outside by
which I mean that Gertrude is meaning and
I am meaning but different and not the same
as opposed to being not the same and
different because differences in meaning are
negatives the same as rain and fish are
negative but not the absolute negative of
nothing which is more and not less negative
than Gertrude who is everything.

E. A. I. MAUNDERS

MOSS

Sound is elliptical
Sorrow is sound
Sorrow is round
Curved like a ball
David and Saul
Knew about sorrow

Pain is a thing
Pieces of string
Tie them together
Wondering whether
Death is away

Thank you for nothing
Take it away
Over the hills

Back to beginning
Lying and sinning
Laughing and loving
Pushing and shoving.

E. A. I. MAUNDERS

CURVE IN CURVE OUT

CATCH Time with a net
Nor yet embrace eternity
Like thin flute notes
Beads in ether—skipping down
Short stubby streets at evening
Without the vulnerable heel
Dr. Juno's Anvils
Babying Gods with comforters
And small edged clouds to ride
And jelly in sand the sea had left
Causing mirth in the basement kitchen
And making foolish extra editions
Trackless dust leaves no tracks
But animals know
And yet we do not know
Beyond small imagery
The history of the crooked stars
And wildly breaking light.

E. A. I. MAUNDERS
        TO F. TENNYSON JESSE

∾

CHURCH OF ENGLAND

GERTRUDE loves the Church of England
Font and Pew and Font
Hassock and Cassock and me
Pulpit pains are Gertrude
Gertrude is Ancient and Modern
And new and old.
Gertrude loves the Church of England
Choristers and boots and Adam's apples
Where through coloured saints sun dapples
Gertrude's cheek and hat bird
Gertrude's big umbrella
All the responses
Candles in sconces
Gertrude loves the Church of England.

Tao Lang Pee

CHANNING AND OLIVE WENCE. TRANSLATORS OF TAO LANG PEE

TAO LANG PEE

❧

INTRODUCTORY NOTE

Born Twang Ko[1]   B.C. 403
Moved to Pakhoi[2]   B.C. 398 or 399
Next heard of Tonkin[3] B.C. 360
And presumably died there.

1 NOTE.—Puriot seems sceptical and on page 2 announces definitely that Tao Lang Pee was not a man at all but the name of an obscure native sexual rite.

2 NOTE.—Professor Pung on the other hand in *The Bean Tree* and *Lotus Lotus*, Royal Geographical Society, Number 486 XLVIII, states absolutely definitely that Tao Lang Pee is still quoted in Thibet.

[1] See Dr. Ruben Field's *China*, page 218.
[2] See Maureen Dangerfield's *Up the Yangtse*.
[3] See Puriot's *Le Chine*.

TAO LANG PEE

❧

" SAMPAN "

WAVES lap lap
Fish fins clap clap
Brown sails flap flap
Chop sticks tap tap
Up and down the long green river
Ohè ohè lanterns quiver
Willow branches brush the river
Ohè ohè lanterns quiver
Waves lap lap
Fish fins clap clap
Brown sails flap flap
Chop sticks tap tap

TAO LANG PEE

꙾

THE EMPEROR'S DAUGHTER

THERE she sits
Wao Ping
With her gold nails
Scratching memories
Lacquer memories of other days
Other lovers
Chow Ho of the casual limbs
Oo Sang Po of the almond teeth and sweet
  breath
Plong How of the short legs and careful
  eyes
There she sits
Wao Ping
In her scarlet Pavilion
Watching the gold carp mouths
Opening tremulously
Dying of love

Because it is Spring in the Lotus Pool
And Spring's lute is cracked
Cracked and broken with too many tunes
Love songs long since sung.

TAO LANG PEE

THE VOICE IN THE BAMBOO SHOOT

THE water is silver
Gliding softly by the Lotus pool
Softly softly softly softly softly
Little Princess Li Chung Ho
Daughter of a thousand stars
Imprisoned in an azure bowl
Where oh where is your lover
Your warrior lover
Lithe and tall helmeted for battle
Helmeted for honourable death
While you wait in your lacquer Pavilion
Tears dropping through the lattice
Tears like the jewels of Mei Tang Poo.

Serge Lliavanov

SERGE LLIAVANOV

SERGE LLIAVANOV

❧

INTRODUCTORY NOTE

IN writing of Serge Lliavanov it is hard to repress a shudder at the cruelty of a Fate which, when he was but four years old, struck him down and left him a hopeless cripple for the remainder of his brief and pain-ridden life. His mother, to whom he was devoted, died when he was five, and his father was exiled to Siberia two years later. Strange to think of the robust gaiety of *The Inn at Tobolsk*, *Kasha* and *The Cossacks' Ride*, emanating from that wasted diseased racked body. In 1915, just before he went blind he wrote *Freedom*, selected excerpts from which are included in this volume. He lived to see his dream of a Soviet administration realised and died peacefully in 1922.

SERGE LLIAVANOV

❧

EVERY DAY

IVAN is lost in the snow
The wolves are howling.
Each bough bends beneath its weary load
Maria Ivanovitch rocks
Rocks by the fire and weeps
Ivan is lost in the snow
In the Nevsky Prospect the snow has been
   cleared away
To allow the Droshkys to pass
Over towards Oomsk the sky is red
Ivan went out with a basket
And swiftly became lost in the snow
In the squares of the city
And in the taverns
There is warmth by the stoves
And good wine
And the thick stocky women of the people

With strong square breasts
And jolly red cheeks
Red as the sky in Oomsk
And sturdy legs,
But Maria Ivanovitch rocks
Rocks by the fire endlessly
Ivan went out with a basket
And was immediately lost in the snow.

SERGE LLIAVANOV

∾

THEATRE PARTY

HERE we are. Programme quickly
Sit yourselves down
The Play begins
See the funny man
How he pretends to be hurt
No No Life is not so easy
Chocolate Panskys[1] for the asking
Delicious are they not
To while away the time
Before the funny man cometh again
To teach us to laugh at sorrow
Ha-ha-ha—ha-ha-ha—
Ho-ho-ho—ho-ho-ho.

[1] Pansky—small heavy doughnut.

SERGE LLIAVANOV

HARLOT'S SONG

Buy me. Buy me. Cheerio. Tip Top.
I will please you
With my happy laughter
And my gay Butterfly ways
Now bold now timid
How you will laugh to see me.
Run from you in mock fear
And then back again
Now sprite now woman
Which will you choose ?
Buy me.   Buy me.
Love is cheap to-day
Because fish must be bought at the market
Haddocks strong and fine
Small tender mussels for my mother
Buy me.   Buy me.
I am young am I not
Young and gay.   Cheerio.   Tip Top.

I will please you.
You cannot buy my heart
That belongs elsewhere
In the trees and mountains and streams
In the deep valleys
My heart is not for sale
It belongs to Michael Michaelovitch
And he is dead
And never again will I see him
Because he is so dead.
But my heart is with him
Under the thick warm earth
You cannot buy my heart
Bid what you will
But I will sing for you
See and dance for you
A dance of old days
One two three so
One two three so
There does that not please you
Buy me.   Buy me.
Cheerio.   Tip Top.

Juana Mandragágita

JUANA MANDRAGÁGITA

JUANA MANDRAGÁGITA

※

INTRODUCTORY NOTE

It was Lawton Drift who just discovered Juana Mandragágita in Granada where she was living with two old ladies. The following year he brought her to Paris and installed her permanently in a small flat in the Rue des Saint Pères. In 1928 she went to Italy for a few days but was soon back again and working as diligently as ever.

I think it can safely be said that the years 1927 to 1929 comprised her Rhythmic Period. Later she forsook rhythm for the " Gothic," "Flamenco" (contained in this volume), belongs to this period together with " Que Verguenza " and " Cuidado Juanita ".

She is now at work on a book of Mallorcine legends which she hopes will be completed by the Spring of 1933.

JUANA MANDRAGÁGITA
Translated by Lawton Drift.

PICNIC NEAR TOLEDO

LIFE is a moment
A moment of life
Is Life giving
Life loving
Life is love
Love loving
Love giving
Cathedrals rotting
In hot sunlight
Mellowing for Death
Death giving
Death loving
Death loving Life
Life loving Death
Why are we waiting
Why sigh

JUANA MANDRAGÁGITA

Why cry
Why cry
Why sigh
Why sigh cries
Why cry sighs
Death Death Death.

JUANA MANDRAGÁGITA

Translated by Lawton Drift

❧

"FLAMENCO"

Ohè Ohè
La—a—aňňa
Lacalacalacalaca—aňň—aňňa
Nyah Nyah
Carista Carista Caristagarcon
Baňero
Paňero
Carista Carista Caristagarcon.

JUANA MANDRAGÁGITA
Translated by Lawton Drift

TORERO

Bull Blood
Blood Bull
Red Red
Hola Hola
Gallant Parade
Ladies and Laces
Voluptuous faces
Music is played
Bull Blood
Blood Bull
Red Red
Hola Hola

Crispin Pither

CRISPIN PITHER

CRISPIN PITHER

❧

INTRODUCTORY NOTE

CRISPIN PITHER was born in Balacorry in 1892. His childhood was more or less normal, the childhood of a little Irish country boy chock-a-block with " fey " legends and superstitions, the traces of which are to be found to-day even in his most realistic and mature works. It was when he was twenty-two that he finally fell out with the Catholic Church. In 1915 he joined an Anti-Catholic organisation in Dublin which flourished but briefly. In 1917 he was at the head of the Anti-Catholic riots in Lausanne which might have had serious consequences for him had he not, by a strange dispensation of Providence, fallen suddenly ill and been forced to take to the mountains. There in almost ascetic seclusion he wrote his Trilogy

Sacrament which was never published. In 1922 he organised an Anti-Catholic Club in Seville which at the beginning gave great promise of success, but later gradually lost hold and was completely extinct by April 1923. His early ballads were mostly written between 1920 and 1924.

In 1925 he was back in Dublin organising an Anti-Catholic mission for Manchuria, a scheme which ultimately fell to the ground owing to lack of support.

In 1927 he wrote *The Village Green* and *Peat*. The excerpts in this volume are from the following :

" Pastoral." *Early Ballads*. Vol. 2
" Deidre." *The Village Green*.
" The Whisht Paple." *Peat*.

CRISPIN PITHER

" DEIDRE "

Deidre the sorrowful smile of you
Deidre the Spring sweet guile of you
Calls me back when the red sun's failin'
Calls me back like a sea-bird wailin'.
Deidre the hard hard heart of you
Maybe the Banshee's part of you
From County Kerry to County Clare
I smell the smell of your tangled hair.

CRISPIN PITHER

"THE WHISHT PAPLE"

As I were lolloping down the lane
On Michael Mulligan's Mary Jane
I spied a whisht man all in green
Bedad says I, 'tis a Ragaleen.
I lolloped on wid a troubled mind
Shure the Davil himself was close behind
Now Father Snuffy I chanced to see
"Mother of Jaysus," says I to he,
"The wee whisht paple are near at hand."
So he drew a circle in the sand
And squatted down in his cassock green
To make a mock o' the Ragaleen.
"Begorrah," says I, "'tis all in vain
The Davil himself is home again,
So climb the Tower and ring the bell
For all of the souls you've prayed to hell."

Then Father Snuffy on bended knee
Strangled himself wid his Rosary
And there where a minute ago had been
A Holy Priest, was a Ragaleen!

CRISPIN PITHER

⁊

" PASTORAL "

" Ah, wheer are ye goin' Macushla Macree?"
Wid a toss o' her curls she's replyin'
" Och, I'm climbin' the mountain to Bally
   Macbog
Wheer me grandmother Bridget is dyin'
Wid a maringadoo aday
And a maringadoo ' adaddy o '."

" And whin you're returnin', Macushla
   Macree
Is it niver a present you're bringin' ? "
" Och, I'll bring ye a part of me grand-
   mother's heart
An' the part that I'm bringin' is singin'
Wid a maringadoo aday
And a maringadoo ' adaddy o '."

" And what if you stay there, Macushla
   Macree
An' lave me this soide of the water ? "
" Och, I'll lave you the pigs and jolly white
   legs
O' Father O'Flannigan's daughter."
Wid a maringadoo aday
And a maringadoo ' adaddy o '."

Albrecht Drausler

ALBRECHT DRAUSLER

ALBRECHT DRAUSLER

❧

INTRODUCTORY NOTE

ALBRECHT DRAUSLER was born in Breslau in 1914. In 1918 his family moved to Fribourg taking him with them. In 1919 he wrote his first poem "Die Armen" (The Poor). In 1920 came *Herren un Damen* and *Aufschnitt*, both works heavy with portent and strangely mature. School-days commenced in 1922, stormy school-days indeed. In 1924 he bicycled to Frankfurt and wrote *Liebes Kind*. The last two lines of which will always be remembered. "Thick hands that clawed my waiting heart, sex hands that pulled me over Death." Fetched back to school he was moody and impatient with his masters. In an extract from Professor Schneider's report in 1926 we read: "Drausler is brilliant in his studies but disappears for long periods, we are at a loss to know what to do with the boy."

In 1928 he wrote his first novel, 250,000 words in length, entitled *Tag*. This was subsequently publicly burnt in Strasbourg.

In 1929 he wrote *Brüderschaft*, three poems from which have been selected for this anthology. In 1930 he opened his veins and died in the school bathroom in Berne, fragments of his last poem " Leben und Tranen " on odd bits of paper littering the floor.

ALBRECHT DRAUSLER
(GEMÜTLICHKEIT)

·ℛ·

FIRST LOVE

LISA's eyes were full of trouble
When she looked at me last Sunday.
Girl's trouble
Her face was blotched and shiny
Where the tears had trickled.
She said she must go down to the Willows
Where we loved.
I do not understand girl's trouble
Perhaps I do not understand love
But hot bread I understand
And Apfelstrude and my mother's hot sweet
    belly
When she bends over in the abendstunde
And says " Curly head my Krochlein "
I asked her yesterday why Lisa had hanged
    herself

Down by the willows.
" Girl's trouble," she said, " Girl's trouble
Curly head my Krochlein."
Perhaps I do not understand girl's trouble.

ALBRECHT DRAUSLER

❧

FREUNDSCHAFT

I WILL wear your cap
If you will wear my cap
I will give you raspberries
If you will give me raspberries.
I will caress your body
If you will caress my body
I will give you a sabre cut
If you will give me a sabre cut
I cannot give you my boots
Because Fritz loves them so
When I have a wife I will give her to you
And you will give me your heart
But not all of it. Just a slice of it
Because of memories and Heinrich
And Spring snows on Eisenthal.

ALBRECHT DRAUSLER

"YOUTH"

FRANZI is fair and Gretchen is dark
And Marlchen's hair is like the Farmer's
boy at home
But all heads are alike against the dark Osiers
Karl's head caught the flame of the dying
sun
When I kissed his mouth
But it was redder when he came out of the
Professor's room
The Frau Professorin was red too
When she pulled Gretchen to her
Why does Herr Dornpfner look at me like
that
When he talks of München
In the Geography lesson
Yesterday there was hay on his waistcoat
Why does everything remind me of the
Farmer's boy?

Jane Southerby Danks

JANE SOUTHERBY DANKS

JANE SOUTHERBY DANKS

༄

INTRODUCTORY NOTE

In writing an introductory preface to Jane Southerby Danks it is odd to compare her early environment with that of her artistic contemporaries. Born in Melton Mowbray in 1897 she rode to hounds constantly, wet or fine, from the age of four onwards. Blauie's portrait " Musette on Roan " depicts her at the very beginning of her adolescence. From the first she shunned the company of the male sex, mixing only with her governesses. To one of whom Madeleine Duphotte she dedicated her first volume of Poems, *Goose Grass*. The Dedication is illuminating in its profound simplicity— " To you, Madeleine, from me."

Storm clouds in her relations with her mother began to gather on the horizon as

early as 1912, indeed in the May of this
year we find her in Florence with Hedda
Jennings then at the height of her career.
Her emancipation from home ties continued
and the breach had obviously broadened
in 1916 when we find her writing from a
whaler off Helsinforth to Mrs. Hinton
Turner (Libelulle) at Saint Cloud. "How
I envy you in your green quiet room. Here,
no lace no Sheffield plate, only tar and the
cry of gulls, but my heart is easier."

1924 finds her cosily ensconced in Bou-
logne where she first gained from the
fisher-folk the appellation " Knickerbocker
Lady."

In 1925 she published *Hands Down* to be
followed in the Spring of 1926 by *Frustration*.

In 1927 began her most prolific era in
Saint Tropey where in company with Zale
Bartlett and Thèrese Mauillac she wrote in
French her celebrated *Coucher de soleil pour
violon* and *Loup de mer*.

The poems included in this volume are
selected from her work of 1929–1930 just
after her quarrel with La Duchesse de la

Saucigny-Garonette (The " Madame Prac-
tique " of " Bon Jour ") and expressing in
their concrete outline her revulsion of
feeling against the Sous Realist School.

JANE SOUTHERBY DANKS

❧

LEGEND

Slap the cat and count the spinach
Aunt Matilda's gone to Greenwich
Rolling in a barrel blue
Harnessed to a Kangaroo
Pock-marked Ulysses approaches
Driving scores of paper coaches
Eiderdowns and soda-water
What a shame that Mrs. Porter
Lost her ticket for the play
(Aunt Matilda's come to stay)
Prod the melons, punch the grapes
See that nobody escapes.
Tea is ready, ting-a-ling
Satan's bells are echoing
Father's like a laughing Ox
Mimsying a paradox

JANE SOUTHERBY DANKS

Aunt Matilda's pet canary
Freda, Sheila, Bob and Mary
All combine to chase the bed
Now that Aunt Matilda's dead.

JANE SOUTHERBY DANKS

SICILIAN STUDY

Dust
Lava
An old man
Two fish baskets
Tarentella Tarentella
Have you seen my blue umbrella?
Fanny left it on the beach
Out of reach, out of reach.
Careless Fanny, careless Fanny
Come to Granny, come to Granny.
Dust
Lava
Peppermint chimes
Dither through the valley
The Campanile totters
In yesterday's gentility.

JANE SOUTHERBY DANKS

❧

RICHMOND BOATING SONG

APPLES and cheese
Come hold my hand
Trip it, Miss Jenkins, to Kew
The Wooden horse is panting—O !
But that's no argument
Look at Frank.
They brew good beer at the " Saucy Sheep "
With a derry dun derry and soon may be
One for all and all for one.
Parrots are blue in old Madrid
And barking tigers screech the song
Rum Tiddy, rum Tiddy
Peculiar.

JANE SOUTHERBY DANKS

OLD THINGS ARE FAR THE BEST

OLD things are far the best
So measure compound interest
On all infirm relations
And let them wait at stations
And never catch the train of Life
Through being too immersed
In conning passion's Bradshaws with " der-
      rieres " reversed
Toward the World of Strife.
So cherish Aunty Amy
And dear old Uncle Dick
And think of Mrs. Roger-Twyford-Mac-
      namara-Wick
Who bicycled to Southsea
When over eighty-two
And never left the handle bars
To contemplate the view.

Though Grandmamma may dribble
Don't point at her and laugh
She gave you Auntie Sybil
A train and a giraffe——
Old things are far the best.

Ada Johnston

ADA JOHNSTON

ADA JOHNSTON

๖๏

INTRODUCTORY NOTE

NOTHING whatever is known about Ada Johnston.

ADA JOHNSTON

༫

THE NURSEMAID

I WISH to bathe my feet in the Turgid Stream
    of Life
And catch the cherry blossoms as they fall
One, two, one two.
The dreams that men have made
Live on in Tunnels underground
I think
A sword to the web of destiny
Would be a comfort in the winter months.
Parrot sound is angular
And wicked edges of the glass people
Crushed insensate
Have rattled like the tin of stones
Designs are futile
Why parody the inevitable
With mystic cherubim, afloat in treacle
By the Norfolk Broads.

ADA JOHNSTON

SUNBURN

MABEL, Mabel,
How blue you are and yet how tawny brown
Your aspidistra feet are soft
And firm as oft
They pound my consciousness
To plastic emptyness.
But I shall borrow matches from the moon
When it is Easter Day.

ADA JOHNSTON

TO RUDYARD KIPLING

TROLL cried the wind
Troll cried the sea
Troll cried the Emperor
What price me.
Thrilling to the touch of your wet, wet
    hands
(Abaft, belay, adjust the boom)
A little wind goes trickling through
The sunset unfurls like Madeira cake
Inviolable the Sanctuary
With a dish and a dash and the scuppers full
Throw the cook overboard,
He won't play.

ADA JOHNSTON

❧

DAWN

A THOUSAND Thanks my father said
Then flung his collar to the swine
That browse in Andalusia
It was raining that day
But beyond
The sun was carolling athwart the blue
And with a laugh we ran
And plucked the shimmering ropes of
   golden swings
It's wonderful the peace contentment brings
And all the ewes are white again
And stark with misty dew
And angular as sheets of light
Beneath the comet's cloudy vest
Innumerable buttons shine
Like pigs in amber.

FINE WORKS OF FICTION AND NON-FICTION AVAILABLE IN QUALITY PAPERBACK EDITIONS FROM CARROLL & GRAF

☐ Anderson, Nancy/WORK WITH PASSION
$8.95 Cloth $15.95
☐ Appel, Allen/TIME AFTER TIME   Cloth $17.95
☐ Asch, Sholem/THE APOSTLE $10.95
☐ Asch, Sholem/EAST RIVER $8.95
☐ Asch, Sholem/MARY $10.95
☐ Asch, Sholem/THE NAZARENE
$10.95 Cloth $21.95
☐ Asch, Sholem/THREE CITIES $10.50
☐ Asprey, Robert/THE PANTHER'S FEAST $9.95
☐ Athill, Diana/INSTEAD OF A LETTER
$7.95 Cloth $15.95
☐ Babel, Isaac/YOU MUST KNOW EVERYTHING
$8.95
☐ Bedford, Sybille/ALDOUS HUXLEY $14.95
☐ Bellaman, Henry/KINGS ROW $8.95
☐ Bernanos, Georges/DIARY OF A COUNTRY
PRIEST $7.95
☐ Berton, Pierre/KLONDIKE FEVER $10.95
☐ Blanch, Lesley/PIERRE LOTI $10.95
☐ Blanch, Lesley/THE SABRES OF PARADISE$9.95
☐ Blanch, Lesley/THE WILDER SHORES OF LOVE
$8.95
☐ Bowers, John/IN THE LAND OF NYX $7.95
☐ Buchan, John/PILGRIM'S WAY $10.95
☐ Carr, Virginia Spencer/THE LONELY HUNTER:
A BIOGRAPHY OF CARSON McCULLERS $12.95
☐ Chekov, Anton/LATE BLOOMING FLOWERS
$8.95
☐ Conot, Robert/JUSTICE AT NUREMBURG$10.95
☐ Conrad, Joseph/SEA STORIES $8.95
☐ Conrad, Joseph & Ford Madox Ford/THE INHERITORS
$7.95

- [ ] Conrad, Joseph & Ford Madox Ford/ROMANCE
  $8.95
- [ ] Cooper, Lady Diana/AUTOBIOGRAPHY $12.95
- [ ] de Montherlant, Henry/THE GIRLS $11.95
- [ ] de Poncins, Gontran/KABLOONA $9.95
- [ ] Edwards, Anne/SONYA: THE LIFE OF COUNTESS
  TOLSTOY $8.95
- [ ] Elkington, John/THE GENE FACTORY Cloth $16.95
- [ ] Farson, Negley/THE WAY OF A TRANSGRESSOR
  $9.95
- [ ] Feutchwanger, Lion/JEW SUSS $8.95 Cloth $18.95
- [ ] Feutchwanger, Lion/THE OPPERMANS $8.95
- [ ] Feutchwanger, Lion/SUCCESS $10.95
- [ ] Fisher, R.L./THE PRINCE OF WHALES
  Cloth $12.95
- [ ] Ford Madox Ford & Joseph Conrad/THE
  INHERITORS $7.95
- [ ] Ford Madox Ford & Joseph Conrad/ROMANCE
  $8.95
- [ ] Fuchs, Daniel/SUMMER IN WILLIAMSBURG
  $8.95
- [ ] Gold, Michael/JEWS WITHOUT MONEY $7.95
- [ ] Goldin, Stephen & Sky, Kathleen/THE BUSINESS
  OF BEING A WRITER $8.95
- [ ] Green, Julian/DIARIES 1928–1957 $9.95
- [ ] Greene, Graham & Hugh/THE SPY'S BEDSIDE
  BOOK $7.95
- [ ] Hamsun, Knut/MYSTERIES $8.95
- [ ] Hawkes, John/VIRGINIE: HER TWO LIVES $7.95
- [ ] Haycraft, Howard (ed.)/THE ART OF THE
  MYSTERY STORY $9.95
- [ ] Haycraft, Howard (ed.)/MURDER FOR PLEASURE
  $10.95
- [ ] Ibañez, Vincente Blasco/THE FOUR HORSEMEN
  OF THE APOCALYPSE $8.95
- [ ] Jackson, Charles/THE LOST WEEKEND $7.95
- [ ] James, Henry/GREAT SHORT NOVELS $11.95
- [ ] Lansing, Alfred/ENDURANCE: SHACKLETON'S
  INCREDIBLE VOYAGE $8.95
- [ ] Leech, Margaret/REVEILLE IN WASHINGTON
  $11.95
- [ ] Linder, Mark/THERE CAME A PROUD BEGGAR
  Cloth $18.95

- Rechy, John/BODIES AND SOULS
$8.95 Cloth $17.95
- Richelson, Hildy & Stan/INCOME WITHOUT TAXES   Cloth $16.95
- Rowse, A.L./HOMOSEXUALS IN HISTORY$9.95
- Roy, Jules/THE BATTLE OF DIENBIENPHU$8.95
- Russel, Robert A./WINNING THE FUTURECloth $16.95
- Russell, Franklin/THE HUNTING ANIMAL
$7.95
- Salisbury, Harrison/A JOURNEY OF OUR TIMES
$10.95
- Scott, Evelyn/THE WAVE $9.95
- Service, William/OWL $8.95
- Sigal, Clancy/GOING AWAY $9.95
- Silverstein, Fanny/MY MOTHER'S COOKBOOK
Cloth $16.95
- Singer, I.J./THE BROTHERS ASHKINAZI $9.95
- Sloan, Allan/THREE PLUS ONE EQUALS BILLIONS $8.95
- Stein, Leon/THE TRIANGLE FIRE $7.95
- Taylor, Peter/IN THE MIRO DISTRICT $7.95
- Tolstoy, Leo/TALES OF COURAGE AND CONFLICT $11.95
- Wassermann, Jacob/CASPAR HAUSER $9.95
- Wassermann, Jacob/THE MAURIZIUS CASE $9.95
- Werfel, Franz/THE FORTY DAYS OF MUSA DAGH $9.95
- Werth, Alexander/RUSSIA AT WAR 1941–1945
$15.95
- Wilmot, Chester/STRUGGLE FOR EUROPE $12.95
- Zuckmayer, Carl/A PART OF MYSELF $9.95

Available from fine bookstores everywhere

To order direct from the publishers please send check or money order including the price of the book plus $1.75 per title for postage and handling. N.Y. State Residents please add 8¼% sales tax.

Caroll & Graf Publishers, Inc.
260 Fifth Avenue, N.Y., N.Y. 10001